"You're a dangerou... murmured

"Me? I can't even hit the target when we practice."

"Don't kid yourself." He ran his hands over her curves. "You've got one hell of an arsenal."

"I'd feel a lot better if I could shoot straight," Christie said with a sigh.

"You'll learn. I'll teach you."

"That's not actually what I want to learn right now," she whispered, snuggling closer.

He kissed her again. Slow, deep. Thorough.

She took the opportunity to undo his jeans and push them down as far she could without stopping the kiss. Boone took over, kicking away his pants to join the rest of his clothes.

Christie stared at his large, muscular body—hard in all the right places. She had to give it to the U.S. Army. They knew how to make their men hot as hell.

Boone could protect her from anything.

Including herself?

Dear Reader,

When I first started writing for Silhouette/Harlequin, I wrote romantic-suspense novels. Then I sashayed over to romantic comedy, which was too much fun. After a while Harlequin Blaze came into my life, and it was hip, urban comedy with oodles of yummy, squirm-in-your-seat sensuality.

Now, with *Closer*... I've combined my two favorite things—heart-pounding suspense with scorching-hot sex! Does it get any better than that?

Closer... takes place in my old stomping grounds—Los Angeles, where ordinary Christie Pratchett is trapped in extraordinarily dangerous circumstances and learns that she can kick ass with the best of them. It doesn't hurt that she's got sexy Boone Ferguson at her side...and in her bed. I mean, who hasn't had a Forbidden Fantasy of taming a mysterious lover from out of the shadows, ready to do *whatever it takes* to keep her safe—and make her his.

Boone, with secrets of his own, leads Christie into a world she never imagined, one she'll continue to explore in my upcoming Harlequin Blaze series, starting with *Relentless* in November 2006.

Now, curl up somewhere warm and safe, and don't forget to lock the doors as you get—*Closer*....

With love,

Jo Leigh

P.S. Check out my Web site at www.joleigh.com.

CLOSER...
Jo Leigh

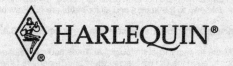

HARLEQUIN®

TORONTO • NEW YORK • LONDON
AMSTERDAM • PARIS • SYDNEY • HAMBURG
STOCKHOLM • ATHENS • TOKYO • MILAN • MADRID
PRAGUE • WARSAW • BUDAPEST • AUCKLAND

ISBN-13: 978-0-373-79269-6
ISBN-10:   0-373-79269-7

CLOSER...

Copyright © 2006 by Jolie Kramer.

This edition published by arrangement with Harlequin Books S.A.

® and TM are trademarks of the publisher. Trademarks indicated with
® are registered in the United States Patent and Trademark Office, the
Canadian Trade Marks Office and in other countries.

www.eHarlequin.com

Printed in U.S.A.

ABOUT THE AUTHOR

Jo Leigh has written over thirty novels for Harlequin and
Silhouette Books since 1994. She's a double RITA® Award
finalist, and was part of the exciting Harlequin Blaze
launch. She also teaches writing in workshops across the
country.

Jo lives high on a mountain in Utah with her wonderful
husband and their new puppy, Jessie. You can chat with
her at her Web site, www.joleigh.com, and don't forget to
check out her daily blog!

Books by Jo Leigh
HARLEQUIN BLAZE

Don't miss any of our special offers. Write to us at the
following address for information on our newest releases.

Harlequin Reader Service
U.S.: 3010 Walden Ave., P.O. Box 1325, Buffalo, NY 14269
Canadian: P.O. Box 609, Fort Erie, Ont. L2A 5X3

To Deb and Dotes—couldn't have done it without ya!
And, as always, to Birgit, for everything.

1

CHRISTIE SAT IN THE FAR CORNER of her living room with her back jammed against the wall. Milo, her golden Lab, whined softly against her as she stared at the phone on the end table, willing the ringing to stop.

How had he gotten the unlisted number? She'd only had that phone for two days. It was her third new number in five months, but the bastard who was stalking her hadn't skipped a beat.

The first phone call had come five months ago. She hadn't recognized the voice. Male. Low. Taunting. She'd hung up, dismissing him as an annoying but inconsequential crank. Right.

Milo rubbed his head against her arm, and she rubbed him back. "You're all right, kiddo," she whispered, blessing him a hundred times. He was the only one left.

The ringing finally stopped. She wondered if she'd ever hear that sound again without terror taking over.

A moment later, the phone rang again, and this time, he left a message. The same message. *You can run, but you can't hide.* The same voice, electronically altered with no background sound but a dull hum. For all she knew, it was a machine calling, and the bastard was outside her house even now, watching her.

The thing was, she'd done everything right. She'd contacted the police, who'd had her log his calls, put up security cameras, tried to trace his calls. She'd hired not one, but two private detectives who'd found out a lot about her neighbors and associates, but all that did was make her afraid of everyone. She'd taped his calls. She'd talked to the FBI, who had assured her that as soon as they had any evidence at all, they'd be all over it.

She'd read books, checked sources on the Internet, had asked for help from everyone she could think of, and still, the bastard was controlling her life.

This was it, though. She couldn't take one more night of this torment. Tomorrow, she was going to call a Realtor, put the house up for sale. But she wouldn't wait around. She'd go to the bank first thing and pull out her savings. She'd take Milo with her and leave. To where, she didn't know or care. Somewhere small. Where he couldn't find her.

Tears filled her eyes, and she didn't even try to blink them back. Her life had gone to hell in the past five months. Everything she cared about had been stripped away, bit by bit.

She'd worked for one of the biggest design firms in Century City, where she'd had clients who ranged from studio executives to movie stars. She'd won awards for her interior designs, but more than that she'd loved her job.

He'd taken that from her last week. She'd been called into the big office and, with a lot of apologies and excuses, her bosses said the reason they were letting her go was because they were refocusing the objectives of the design firm. She'd come right out and asked if they'd been threatened, and while they'd denied it, Kerry and Stanley had both gotten so nervous and upset that she knew the stalker had somehow gotten to them. Her certainty had convinced the police to investigate, but they hadn't gotten the couple to talk. The bastard had scared them spitless.

She had no business being so angry. She understood the fear. But she *was* angry. And achingly disappointed.

She went over to the pad of paper by the phone. Her log covered so many pages it was starting to resemble the L.A. phone book. On it, she recorded every incident, from e-mail threats to inappropriate gifts, to the content of messages left on her machine. She wrote it all down. The date, time, place and description. There was a space to notate witnesses, but there were none. Still, the police could do nothing. Would do nothing. Even with the anti-stalking laws in place, the bastard was so clever he never let them get anything on him. The FBI had traced the e-mail messages, but ended up with a variety of dead ends. Tracing his calls had proved equally unsuccessful. He was using either a cloned or a prepaid cell, neither of which could be traced.

The packages that had showed up on her doorstep had been searched for clues, but not a fingerprint had been found. As for the security cameras…they'd been a complete bust. Not one picture, not even a shadow.

Locks had proven useless. It didn't matter that they were guaranteed to be the latest technology and completely burglar-proof, he got through them. He got into her house. Left messages. One on her bathroom mirror, in her own lipstick. *You can run but you can't hide.* Two days ago, he'd eaten a piece of cake from her fridge.

He'd tranquilized Milo, which had scared her to death. Because if the tranquilizer hadn't worked, she had no doubt he would have killed her dog.

She'd stopped asking the obvious question long ago. There was no reason behind this. Just because she didn't recognize his voice didn't mean she didn't know him. He could be anyone. Her best friend's husband. The man across the street. Anyone.

So she'd crawled into her house, once her pride and joy, until it had become a prison. If she didn't break out tomorrow, it would become her coffin.

"Come on, baby," she said, standing up. "Let's get you fed."

Christie had lost almost ten pounds since it began. Her skin was pale, her hands shook. She'd stopped bothering with makeup, kept putting her hair back in a messy ponytail, and she always wore shoes she could run in. She was under siege and he never let her forget it.

As she headed for the kitchen, she glanced at her mantel, at the picture of Nate. He would have helped her. Her big brother was ex-Delta Force. He would have caught the bastard and damn quick. But Nate was dead, and that wound was still raw.

She got out Milo's bowl and his food. The irony of her situation wasn't lost on her. She'd never had patience for the victim mentality. She believed in movement, in taking charge, in handling things. Never one to back down, she'd fought for her college grades, kicked ass at work, bought her own home, never settled when it came to men. And here she was, a pitiful, terrified shadow who hadn't slept a full night in months.

She finished fixing Milo's dinner, and put it in his spot at the end of the island. Milo, unlike herself, still had his appetite. She sighed as she went to the fridge. The last time she'd eaten was...hell, she had no idea. So maybe forcing some food wasn't a bad idea.

A couple of scrambled eggs was all she could handle. She ate standing by the stove. Milo had finished and was expecting his walk, which was something she couldn't avoid. Instead of taking him around the block, or even to the park that was five blocks away, she would drive to a random location. Somewhere crowded. Last night had been Melrose Avenue. The night before, Westwood Boulevard. Tonight, she'd go west. Santa Monica. Not that it mattered. He could be following her car. He could be in the house five minutes after she left. He could kill her in her sleep.

The phone made her jump, and she almost dropped her plate. Dammit, she should have unplugged it. Who was this guy? How in hell did he know so much about her life? He'd even gotten to her book club.

They used to meet at the bookstore every other Wednesday. But then the women started getting notes on their windshields. Two of them got flat tires. None of her friends had connected the vandalism to her because she hadn't told them about the bastard. But she knew. So she quit. They'd all believed her lame excuse, which was a relief, because she wouldn't be able to stand it if he hurt someone she knew.

"Milo? You ready?"

He clearly was, if jumping around and wagging his butt was anything to go by. Christie didn't even glance at the mirror as she got his leash. She just headed into the garage, all her senses on alert as she turned on the light.

Senses. She didn't have any senses left. Sleep deprivation had made her stupid and reckless, and that made her a fool. It was the house that had held her. Goddammit, she loved her home. It wasn't just the money she'd poured into it, either. She'd made it her cocoon, her safe haven. Every room created for her pleasure and delight.

She locked the car doors after Milo climbed in, and then steeled herself to open the garage door behind her. It went up slowly, her gaze locked on the rearview mirror. The car was running, in reverse, her foot resting on the gas.

The second she was clear, she jammed out, then hit the brake hard when she got to the end of her driveway. A quick check both ways and she pressed the remote for the garage door. Once it was down she tore out again, tires squealing. How she wished he'd been in the way.

"THAT CAN'T BE RIGHT," Christie said, shifting on the blue chair across from the bank's vice president. "I've never had any dispute with the IRS."

Jennifer Abbott, in her nice gray suit with her nice beige nails and her nice practiced smile, looked at her computer screen, then back at Christie. "There's nothing I can do, except advise you to talk to the IRS."

"Please check again. You must have me mixed up with someone else."

Christie watched as the woman typed on her keyboard. She thought about last night, how she'd laid in bed, planning out her move. How she would call the Realtor from a pay phone, take her savings and her dog, and head toward Arizona. There was no plan if there was no money. But he couldn't have gotten to her bank. That was impossible, even for the cleverest stalker. He was just a man. A sick, twisted prick, but still… How could he get the IRS to do his bidding?

"I'm sorry, Ms. Pratchett. All three accounts have been seized and there's nothing at all we can do from here. I'll give you the information they gave us. There's a number you can call."

Christie sat very, very still. Because any second she was going to lose it, and she didn't want to, not here. Not sitting in the bank where she'd been a customer for over twelve years. She'd call the FBI, of course, but even if they did get right on it, it would still take time to clear it up. She had no hope in hell that they'd figure out who was behind this latest horror. That left her with the money in her purse, which wasn't a lot. If she were lucky, her credit cards would still be good, but she doubted it. And that meant…

She had no idea what it meant. That the bastard owned her? That he'd be coming for her now? That he was laughing his ass off, knowing he'd destroyed every inch of her life?

She cleared her throat, unable to stop her body from trembling. "Can you tell me when this was done?"

"Yesterday afternoon."

"I see." Christie stood up, not quite sure her legs would hold her.

"I'm certain everything will work out in the end," Jennifer said, handing her the printout with the IRS information. Then she picked up her phone.

Dismissed, Christie headed back to her car. The drive home was a daze, and when she got into the house she didn't even bother locking the door behind her. She had nothing. Maybe a hundred bucks. Would that even get her out of town?

It had to, because if it didn't, she was going to fall apart, and no one would ever be able to put her back together again.

Of course, Milo was there with his big brown eyes and his wagging tail. She gave him a hug, then she went to her office. Methodically, without even thinking, she opened the drawers and pulled out all the paperwork she'd be taking with her. Passport, insurance, bank records—which probably wouldn't do her any good—and her mortgage papers. Everything went into her briefcase. She did the work carefully, her hands still shaking. She paused when she found a copy of her parents' living wills.

She should head toward Illinois, toward the nursing home where her father lived, if you could call it living. Her mother's apartment near the home was so small there was no room for Christie. They were getting by on so little, her mom had cried when Christie told her she'd lost her job. For years, it had been Christie's money that had provided anything over the bare necessities.

Nate hadn't left much. A small bank account and a motorcycle. The money had gone to Mom and Dad.

Behind the will, she found a picture of Nate in his uniform. God, he'd been a handsome devil. She turned it over and saw a phone number she'd forgotten all about. Not that it would do her any good now.

She remembered when he'd given it to her. Nate's voice was so clear in her head, even now. He'd told her she should call that number if she ever needed help. That if she were ever in trouble, he would come. No matter what.

There was no reason to pick up the phone. He'd been dead seventeen months. But she did, anyway. She picked it up and dialed, and when the man answered on the second ring, she barely heard him say "Gino's Pizza."

"I'm—" She had to clear her throat again, and damn, enough with the tears. "I'm Nate Pratchett's sister."

"No Nate works here, miss."

"You didn't know him?"

"Sorry."

"Everybody's sorry," she said. "Everybody wishes they could help. But they can't."

"Did you want a pie?"

"No. I want help. But you can't do that. Never mind." She hung up.

It took her a long time to move again. In fact, it was Milo to the rescue yet again. He knew. He knew she was in pain, that she was desperate, and in all the world, he was the only one who did a thing. He loved her.

Once she could move again, she started where she'd left off. Going through every piece of paper, taking only the essentials. She thought about bringing her address book, but when she flipped through it, there were only work contacts and the few friends she'd managed to avoid since this began. After the book club fiasco, she'd been scared to let anyone in. Scared she'd get them hurt, or worse.

It was dark when she stood up. Time to feed Milo.

Once again, she went through the motions. Giving Milo his dinner, taking him to another street, this time in Beverly Hills. But driving back, she almost fell asleep, and it was only furious honking from a Hummer that prevented a head-on collision.

So she wouldn't leave tonight. If she could just get a few hours of sleep, it would be okay. She could pack her clothes in the morning. Now, all she wanted was to be home. To get in bed. To please, God, wake up and find out this was all a nightmare.

She got part of her wish. Safely home, she locked everything up, took a fast shower. She put on her most comfortable old T-shirt. It was stretched out and so thin it was held together by hope, but it was soft and it comforted. Then she called her dog and they both climbed into her bed.

As she put her head on the pillow, she stared up at the dark ceiling. Would she ever sleep in this bed again? The sheets had been a splurge, eight hundred thread count. The headboard had been custom-made of cherrywood. Her own design. It was one of the things she loved most about her house. Her bathroom was, too. A shower that had nooks built in for candles. Jerusalem tile she'd picked out piece by piece. The bathtub was oversized with twelve jets and a sound system built into the walls.

She went through a list of all the moments, the decisions, the construction process that led to the dream becoming reality. This was more her home than anywhere she'd ever lived, including her parents' house of her childhood. She'd put her soul into this place, and tomorrow morning she would walk out the door, and she had no faith at all that she would ever come back.

One man had taken her life. It would have been kinder if he'd simply killed her. She'd thought about doing the job herself, but she couldn't go through with it. She'd fought her whole life, she couldn't give up now. Even though she wasn't sure what she was fighting for.

Milo moved, pressing his front paws into her thigh. She welcomed the contact. She'd always loved her pup, but never so much as in the last months. What would she have done without him?

Oddly, that thought led her straight to Nate. Her big brother had been the one to teach her to be strong. Neither of her parents had been. It was Nate who'd taught her not to take any guff from guys. He'd even told her, in a most enlightening and embarrassing afternoon, about sex. He'd been the one who'd walked her to school. Who had helped with her homework. Who had been there for her, always.

And then, he was gone. At the time, she'd thought it was the worst pain she'd ever have to face. Even worse than her father's Alzheimer's. Worse than her mother's obliviousness to most of Christie's life. It still hurt her terribly to think of Nate. Especially now when she needed him the most.

She closed her eyes, vaguely surprised that she wasn't crying. Maybe she didn't have any more tears left. Maybe those had been taken along with her faith in law enforcement, her faith in the whole concept of right and wrong. Everything had changed, and it was all out of her control. No matter how hard she fought, it was tilting at windmills.

She had the clothes on her back. Her car. Milo. She had a degree and a trade. Somehow, she'd claw her way back to her life. If he didn't follow her.

That was a really huge *if.* Just one more thing she didn't have faith in.

Could she live the rest of her life in terror? Did she even want to?

She turned over, clutched her pillow and prayed for sleep.

SHE HAD NO IDEA WHY SHE woke up. Only that Milo wasn't there.

Had she heard something? Her gaze went to the bedside clock. It was one-twenty in the morning, and as she strained to hear, there was only silence.

He'd probably gone out the doggie door to the backyard. Or gone for a drink of water. There was nothing to be worried about, no reason for her heart to pound in her chest and her throat to close with fear. It wasn't the first time she'd freaked out over nothing.

She pushed back the bedcovers anyway, and reached into her bedside drawer to pull out her gun. The one she'd bought three months ago, after the first time the bastard had been in her house. It didn't matter that she'd always been afraid of them. If he was here, he wasn't getting out alive.

The room was dark, but once she got into the hall, the night-light would give her strength. Tiptoeing, her bare feet made no sound as she crossed the hardwood floor to the door.

She paused there, listening again. Nothing. No sound. Wait. It was Milo. His low whine.

If the bastard hurt her dog, she'd shoot off his pecker.

Taking another careful step, she reached the hall. The night-light illuminated the space slightly. It didn't make her feel better. There was no one there, and she was tempted for a moment to go back to her bedroom and lock the door. But she'd never rest until she found out why Milo was whining.

Her heart pounding, she entered the living room. The first thing she saw was her dog, and he was staring. Not at her. Behind her.

She turned and her Glock was ripped from her hand. It banged on the floor, as another hand, his hand, pulled her to his body, her back to his front. As she tried to scream, his hand covered her mouth. Everything was tight and real and she knew this was it. She was going to die.

Milo leapt at the man, but he sidestepped, taking her with him. She willed the dog to bite the bastard right in the balls. Instead, she kicked the man, connecting with his leg. She heard a grunt, and then a voice.

"Stop it," he whispered. "Christie, just stop."

She kicked him again. The bastard wasn't going to take her down without a fight. All the frustration, all the rage she'd held in for so long went directly into the only parts she could still move. She banged back with her head, kicked him again and tried to reach him with her nails.

"Shit, would you stop?" She could feel the muscles in his chest, the strength of his thighs. He was big, and in her stupid sleep-shirt, barefoot, she couldn't hurt him. She also couldn't breathe.

It was the latter that made her still. Time slowed as she grew lightheaded. All she could think was *Please, make it fast. I can't stand pain. Don't hurt me.*

Then darkness. Then nothing.

2

CHRISTIE WOKE. It was her bed, her room, and it was night. As the muddle in her head cleared, she felt her fear surge back full force. It hadn't been a dream. The bastard was here, in her house. She reached over to her bedstand, but the drawer was open and empty. Instead, she grabbed the phone, but there was no dial tone. Tossing it to the bed, she got up, not willing to waste a second panicking. He was here. She had to get out.

Going directly to the window, she tried to open it and couldn't. Of course, she'd locked it. To keep him out. Her shaking fingers couldn't grasp the lock right, and when she finally did, there were the screws above the inside window to pull free. She'd never experienced terror like this, not with any of his phone calls or even the notes he'd left inside. If she didn't get out, she knew she would die.

"What are you doing?"

She spun around at the voice. "Don't come near me."

He stood in the doorway, but all she could see was his silhouette. He was so large. His shoulders nearly filled the space, his head just a few inches from the top. There was something in his hand. A mug. Her coffee mug. "I'm not going to hurt you." He spoke softly. Barely above a whisper.

"You son of a bitch. I'll scream. I'll scream my head off."

"You don't have to do that. I promise. I'm here to help. But please, keep your voice down."

She laughed, but it sounded more like a sob.

"Christie," he said, moving a bit closer. "Your brother sent me."

Her breath caught. "My brother's dead."

"I know. But he gave you a phone number. You called that number this morning."

"What?" she asked, knowing it was a trick.

"I served with Nate," he said, his whisper deeper, as if it wasn't quite real. "He saved my life."

"You could have tapped my phone."

"I could have, but I didn't."

He took a step into the room and Christie backed up, banging her head against the window.

"Hold on. I'll show you." He walked over to her bed and put the mug down on the side table. Then he reached into his back pocket and pulled out his wallet.

Christie watched him, knowing she should make a run for it. Break the window if she had to. Scream, like she'd threatened. But she felt immobilized. As if her feet were stuck to the floor.

He approached, and every muscle in her body tightened. He handed her a snapshot.

Her fingers shook so it was hard to focus. It helped when he turned on the light by her bed. In the photo, she found Nate instantly. He wore camouflage, complete with floppy hat. Next to him was a big guy. The one standing not a foot away. There were other people in the picture, two men and two women. The six of them were smiling. Happy. Their weapons held casually, the way she used to hold her stuffed bear.

"That was in Kosovo. I'm sure Nate told you we were there."

She looked at his face, which she could see clearly for the first time. Like Nate, he was a good-looking man. Dark hair cut short, but not as short as in the picture. Vivid eyes with long, dark lashes. An angular jaw and a full lower lip. He wasn't as tall as she'd thought. Maybe six-two. And while his shoulders were broad, his hips were slim, his legs long. There were small lines at the edges of his eyes and a furrow between his eyebrows. "They said it was a pizza parlor."

"It is. But the man who owns it doesn't just make pizza."

Her hands still shook as she returned the picture. "Why the hell did you break in?"

"I'm sorry about that. I didn't think I'd wake you. I didn't want your stalker to know I was here."

"You know about the stalker?"

He nodded. "I got on it as soon as I heard about your call."

"Got on it? What, you broke into the police department?"

"No. I have someone at the FBI who helped."

"Jesus." She pushed back her hair, wondering if this was the part where the men in the white coats entered. "So, what, you're here to…?"

"Help. To catch him. To make sure he doesn't hurt you."

"The police and the FBI haven't been able to do squat. What makes you so sure you can do anything?"

"Trust me. I can. I've already done a preliminary sweep in here. I found these." He reached into his breast pocket and pulled out a jumble of tiny electronic bits. "Why don't we sit down. Talk this thing through."

She nodded, hardly believing her eyes. The bastard had put bugs in her bedroom? It creeped her out so much her knees nearly buckled. She barely made it to the bed, where she sat for a few minutes remembering how to breathe.

When she was calm enough to talk, she looked up. "What's your name?"

"Boone. Boone Ferguson."

"There are only two possibilities here," she said. "One, you're him, and you've planned this whole thing, including the picture in your wallet. Two, you really did serve with Nate, and for some unknown reason, you want to help. If it's the first, there's not a hell of a lot I can do about it. You win. If it's the second…" The breath she'd fought for slipped away. "You win there, too. I have nothing left. I was going to leave first thing in the morning. But he got to the bank. Had the IRS seize my accounts. I'm broke. I'm tired. I give up."

Boone nodded. "Here's what you're going to do right now. Put on a robe and some slippers, take that mug of tea and come into the kitchen. Give me about ten minutes. I want to make sure we're not overheard."

"Where's Milo?"

Boone almost smiled. "He's in the kitchen. Ten minutes."

She watched him leave. He wore jeans and an oxford shirt with the sleeves rolled up. He could have been a businessman or an architect. In truth, she had no idea who he was. Only that if he were telling the truth, he'd known Nate.

Instead of the robe, she changed into jeans and a shirt. She'd never go to bed in just a T-shirt again. As she dressed, she remembered some letters Nate had sent her from the Balkans. At the first opportunity, she'd get them out, check and see if there were any mention of Boone Ferguson. The name sure didn't ring a bell.

Once she'd dressed, she took the cooled mug into the kitchen where Milo was gnawing on a big rawhide bone. One she hadn't given him.

Boone was at the table, a large duffel bag by his chair and an array of electronic equipment spread before him. He looked up at her, then back at the meter in his hand.

"More bugs?" Those, at least, had convinced her to keep her voice down. Way down.

He nodded. "When was he in here?"

She went to the microwave and stuck the mug in for a minute. As she waited, she turned to him. "The last time was three days ago. He ate cake."

"Ate cake?"

She joined him at the other side of the table. "He also left me a note. It said 'You can run, but you can't hide.' So it's safe to talk now?"

"Let's keep it down, just in case, but I'm pretty sure the room is clean." He looked down at the mess of electronic bits spread out in front of him. "This is some so-phisticated shit."

"Not as sophisticated as his IRS trick."

"I've got someone who might be able to help with that."

"How?"

"He's got...interesting connections. We'll see. Back to the stalker, do you have any idea who he is?"

"No. None."

"He's been after you for what, five months?"

"Yes. He's been relentless. I've gone to the police, the FBI. No one has been able to find out a thing."

"Has he indicated what he wants?"

She stared at him. "Are you kidding?"

"No. Some stalkers are very specific. They're after a relationship, or they believe they've been wronged in some way. If his messages have had any kind of theme, that could be helpful."

"He wants me to be afraid. Hold on," she said, rising. Milo watched her, his paws still guarding his bone, as she went to the living room and got her log book. "Tell me something," she said, handing it to Boone. "What did you do to Milo?"

"I gave him a bone."

"No. Before. He didn't attack you. He just whined." She sat down again. "Like you were the mailman or something. Not an intruder."

"Ah. Yeah, well. I have this spray."

"Pepper spray?" she said, ready to find her gun.

"No, no. Nothing like that. He's fine. Not harmed in any way."

"What kind of spray?"

"It's a gentle tranquilizer. It's already gone from his system."

"You drugged my dog and broke into my house, and I'm having tea with you."

"I told you. I'm here because of Nate."

"Maybe you ought to tell me more about that. A whole lot more."

"I promise, I'll tell you everything I can. But first, I have to finish my sweep. I don't want you saying a word out there until I'm done."

"How long?"

"A few hours. He's clever and he's got great toys. I have to make sure. Christie, not all of these are listening devices. Some are cameras. He had two outside, which I disabled, but I have no idea how many more there could be."

She shivered as she thought about her options. It was hellish being at Boone's mercy, but she'd been at the bastard's mercy for months. Just the fact that he'd been listening… Watching… Christ. In her bedroom.

A wave of nausea made her clutch her stomach. Not that she'd had any action for a billion years, but she wasn't one to shy away from taking care of herself. "What can I do?"

"Get some sleep."

She laughed. "Yeah. That's gonna happen."

He looked at her hard, that furrow between his eyes deep and serious. Green. She hadn't seen that in the bedroom, but his eyes were a dramatic green. They weren't like emeralds, or the grass outside her house. Maybe like the ocean by the pier in Santa Monica.

"Sleep is the thing that will help the most," he said. "It won't be easy, and if you can't fall asleep, you should at least lie down and close your eyes. You're going to need everything in the next few days. All your brains and all your reflexes. If you're too tired, you become a liability instead of an asset. From what I've heard, you're not going to want to sit back and watch. So do us both a favor and go to bed."

Christie felt as though she should be insulted. But that was probably just his tone, not his message. And it wasn't really his tone, because he'd talked in that whisper of his. "You're right. I'm exhausted. Will you wake me when you're finished?"

"I'd rather wait until morning, if you're willing. You could use the rest."

"If I'm still sleeping, then let me sleep," she said. "But whenever I wake up, you're going to tell me what I want to know."

"Yes, ma'am."

"Ma'am. Right." She turned to Milo, who was still having his way with the rawhide bone. She wanted him to come to bed with her, but his chewing would keep her awake, and she didn't have the heart to take the treat away. Instead, she stood up, thought once again that she was quite insane for letting Boone stay in her house, and doubly so for going to sleep while he had the full run of the place. But she was so damn tired, it didn't matter. "There's fruit in the fridge. And stuff to make a sandwich."

"Thank you."

"I threw out the rest of the cake."

He nodded slightly, then went back to examining the

stuff. By the time she reached her bed and turned off the light, she was halfway out. Hitting the pillow was just dumb luck.

BOONE HAD SEEN THIS EQUIPMENT many times. It was top-of-the-line, and mostly unavailable to the public. John Q. Public couldn't get it from the neighborhood spy store, but it could be found. Whoever the stalker was, he knew what he was doing. He'd placed the bugs perfectly—in the smoke detector, in a loose tile by the refrigerator. If Boone hadn't known the ropes he'd have missed at least one.

He got up, stretched and dismissed the idea of getting a sandwich. There was too much to do before Christie woke up. He grabbed his bag, slipped on his night-vision goggles, and headed for her office.

It took over two hours to do the bug sweep. The stalker was inventive, that's for sure. Boone was certain he was someone in security, maybe even a spook, and that made Boone damned uncomfortable. The stalker's obsession most likely had nothing to do with his profession, but it did make him far more dangerous.

Stalkers weren't all the same, but they all had things in common. They were socially immature loners, unable to establish or sustain close relationships. They tended to pick unattainable victims, and create intimate fantasies that could turn deadly in the blink of an eye. Intelligence was a factor, too. Many delusional stalkers were smart as hell, which made catching them more difficult.

Boone had never gone after a stalker before, but he'd had a lot of experience going after people who didn't want to be found.

He sat down at her computer, took off the goggles, then booted up. He'd already found a bug at her desk, but now he was looking for software. Particularly key-logging software. If this guy was a security geek, he would have used his time inside the house to get more access. If he had key-logging technology, he'd be able to read her every keystroke, and see every message she wrote. The more personal the better.

He wouldn't be obvious about it, either. It wouldn't be under the software name. Boone would have to look for hidden files, for specific code. Luckily, he had his own program that did just that. He inserted the disk and let it run. It would take a while, and in the meantime, he could continue with his sweep.

He stood, and his gaze caught on a picture of Nate and Christie, barely illuminated by the light near the computer.

Nate had told him a lot about his sister, but not how beautiful she was. The picture, taken in better times, showed him how much this ordeal had taken out of her. She'd lost weight, which was understandable. But the bones were there. Big brown eyes, dark hair that swept her shoulders. Everything was right about her face, especially her smile. Warm, inviting. He wondered how long it had been since she'd laughed. Since she'd known any peace at all.

He remembered one night, several years ago, when he and Nate were stuck together doing some surveillance in a damp, cold building in the middle of a burned-out Serbian village. There was nothing going on, and nothing to do. They couldn't sleep, so they talked. Nate got on to the subject of Christie. He never talked much about his family, so Boone had paid attention. It was clear Nate loved her, and felt protective of her, but it was equally evident that he was proud of his baby sister. How she'd gotten through college on a scholarship, how she'd become a designer to the stars. The way he described her, as funny and sarcastic, had stuck in Boone's mind long after the conversation and the mission ended.

He'd thought a lot about her after that. He had no one close, except for the men in his unit, so she'd become a comfort to him when things got rough, much as she had for Nate. He'd imagine her at Christmas, when he was stuck in a jungle or a town where he didn't know the language. It wasn't anything sexual, just comforting. But now that he'd seen her, he'd never think of her as a little sister again.

She also reminded him of Nate. The way she lifted her right eyebrow in doubt. Rubbing her lower lip when she was nervous. They were both habits Nate had, ones Boone hadn't consciously noted until seeing them echoed in Christie.

He picked up the photo, studying her, filling in the blanks. Once Seth had sent out the SOS, Boone had used his slippery network of inside sources—some from the military, some from domestic agencies—and found the records of the stalker immediately. He'd spent the next five hours digesting everything he could about the geek. Then he'd come here. He didn't live far—a rented house in Pasadena. It hadn't taken any time to gather his equipment. He always had it packed.

The only problem was the work he'd left behind. He

might be living under the radar, but that didn't mean he wasn't busy. Since he'd come back from the Balkans, he'd found a lot of people who needed his services. Others, like himself, who worked in the shadows, came to him when they had security problems. Someone listening. Someone they needed to listen to. Although he'd been a radioman in Delta, he'd acquired a lot of gadgets and the know-how to get the jobs done.

Seth had stepped up to the plate once more. If anyone knew more about covert surveillance than Boone, it was Seth, and he'd agreed to take over Boone's jobs until the stalking bastard had been taken out. It was a relief to know that despite the mess they were all in, the unit had never lost touch. They were a team, now and always.

Boone moved on. The hallway. The guest bedroom. The back porch. The collection of bugs grew. Most of them were listening devices, but some were also cameras. The freak understood about security grids, so that there were pitifully few places for Christie to hide.

He couldn't wait to get his hands on the prick.

The first hints of daylight were changing the sky when Boone felt as if he could stop. He wasn't finished. He wanted to do more sophisticated tests, but that could wait until he'd caught a few hours of sleep.

Besides, it looked like Milo, who'd been following him from room to room, carrying his mangled bone, wasn't going to rest until he did.

Instead of going to the guest room, which was too far away from the doors, Boone would crash in the living room. He'd left the computer running, his software checking every line of code. By the time he woke up, he should know exactly what the geek had planted.

There was only one more thing he had to do before he could rest. In four different spots in the house, Boone put in four different cameras. His own. Not to spy on Christie, but to catch the geek. Maybe he wouldn't need them, but Boone wasn't a man to take chances. He also put a bug in the phone. If the stalker called again, Boone wanted a record.

After running a quick check to make sure everything was running properly, he went to the living room and decided the couch was too narrow, so he stretched out on the floor. Milo joined him, not touching, but close. Boone closed his eyes, and he was gone.

3

CHRISTIE HEADED TOWARD THE GUEST ROOM, tightening the belt of her robe and wondering just how much of last night was real, when she saw him on the floor.

He was on his back. No pillow, no blanket. Just flat out, his mouth slightly open, his right arm flung across his chest. Milo, who was curled up next to Boone's hip, looked up at her questioningly, as if defending his choice of sleepmates.

Okay, so the Boone part hadn't been a dream. Which meant the bugs and cameras weren't, either.

She headed to the kitchen and got busy making coffee. She felt odd, and not just because of the stranger in her home. After the fourth scoop of Sumatra Mandheling, it dawned on her that she felt rested. Not week-in-a-spa rested, but it was the first morning in ages she could actually see clearly. More than that, the panic that had become her heartbeat was gone. No, not gone. Dampened. Definitely dampened.

In theory, Boone could be the bastard. Somehow, though, she didn't think so. He would have tried something last night. She'd crashed in bed, he'd disabled the phone and she had no weapons. He already knew that if she were too scared, she passed out like a little girl. Instead, he'd gone to sleep on the floor of her living room. She didn't understand that part at all. There was a perfectly nice guest bedroom just down the hall—so, what, he had a bad back?

What she needed was coffee and an explanation. She desperately wanted him to be just what he said he was. It embarrassed her to realize how badly she needed to be rescued. Her, the woman who'd built her life around the fact that she was perfectly capable of taking care of herself. That the knight in shining armor was nothing but a myth. And a destructive one at that.

She poured the water into the coffeemaker and pressed the On button. The gurgle was a welcome sound, as was the click of doggie nails on the bamboo floor. Turning to face a very guilty-looking Milo, she crossed her arms and gave him the glare. "Breakfast time and who loves Mom now, huh? Didn't your new best friend bring kibble, too?"

"Nope. Forgot it."

Christie looked up to find Boone, his hair sticking up and his shirt wrinkled, standing just outside the kitchen.

"Is that coffee?"

"It is."

"You have cream?"

"Milk."

"It'll do. I'll be back." He turned and headed toward the bathroom.

She looked at Milo. "What do you see in him? Besides his big bone?"

Milo wagged his tail, but that was probably more to

do with the fact that she'd picked up his bowl than any prurient interest in Boone.

As she gave Milo his two scoops, she had yet another revelation. She'd made a joke. An admittedly poor joke, but still. Nothing had been funny, not since that first phone call. She put the dog dish down and when she stood, she pushed her hair back. It was longer than she liked it, and she hadn't had highlights in four months. Hair care, along with other nonessentials such as eating and sleeping, had slipped away as she'd been forced into her nightmare existence. Seems, however, that like her sense of humor, she'd discovered she still had some vanity left, and she wished she'd showered before coming into the kitchen.

When Boone joined her, he'd changed into a plain white T-shirt and a faded pair of jeans. Her idea of him as a businessman fell away as he reached down to pet Milo. The muscles of his back strained the shirt, making her wonder how he kept in such good shape. Of course, her gaze shifted downward and his jeans were just tight enough for her to see the curve of his small, tight, high rear end. Not that she had any prurient interest, either.

He stood and she blushed.

"Coffee?"

"Not yet," she said. "I'm going to take a shower. Help yourself. And don't leave. We need to talk."

"I'm not going anywhere," he said.

She headed to her room, curious, concerned, confused. But she couldn't interrogate someone while in her bathrobe. After gathering her clothes, she went into her shower, making the water as hot as she could stand it. She'd had three nozzles installed, not just one, and they hit her in all the right places. Head, upper back, lower back. Perfect to release tension. Maybe today it would do just that.

THE PHONE RANG WHILE SHE WAS in the shower. Boone went to the living room and checked that the answering machine was on. After four rings, the message played— Christie's voice, no nonsense, nothing provocative. Just a request for a name and number after the tone.

The voice he heard after that wasn't so benign. He knew immediately that it was distorted by a digital signal processor, and there was a low electronic hum in the background so that nothing could be traced.

"Naughty girl, Christie. You know we can't let your friend come between us. If he leaves now, he won't get hurt. And neither will you."

There was a click, and then the dial tone. Boone opened the answering machine and lifted out the tape. Despite the tricks the prick had used, Boone was going to let Seth give it a look.

He went back to the kitchen, debating the wisdom of telling Christie about the call. She was upset enough. What she needed now was confidence. The decision made, he went back to his duffel and put the tape in a small bag, ready for Seth. He'd drop it off later.

He poured her a cup of coffee as soon as he heard her in the hallway. He'd already had one, but another wouldn't go to waste. If he was going to be here for a while, he'd have to get to the market. She didn't have much, and he was a stickler for his coffee his way. Besides, she needed to put on some pounds.

She walked in, changed from her robe into a pair of jeans and a blue T-shirt that he guessed used to be her size. The jeans were big, and where the shirt had a V he could see too much bone and not enough flesh. Shopping, definitely. After he'd done another sweep outside. He wasn't taking any chances. By tonight, he'd know everything the geek had planted in or around her house. He'd check out her car, too.

"Is this for me?" She nodded at the mug he'd poured.

"Yeah."

Her look was more suspicious than grateful.

"You had questions?" he asked.

She went to the fridge and got out her low-fat milk, then to the cupboard for a packet of sugar substitute. When the coffee was to her liking, she sat down across from him. "Tell me about you and Nate."

"We met at Fort Bragg. We'd both been recruited into the First Special Forces Operational Detachment, and we trained together. He became a team leader, I was the radioman. There were four of us, basically, and some UN personnel. We were all together in that picture I showed you. We did a lot of hairy missions. Never lost a man. Never fell short of the objective."

"Nate would never tell me what he did. Just that he was working for God and country."

Boone could hear him say just that. In bars, mostly, when he was trying to impress the ladies. As if he'd needed a line. The women fell all over him. Not that Boone had done so badly, but he'd never been the magnet Nate was.

"Why are you smiling?"

He hadn't realized he was. "Just remembering."

Christie leaned forward, and he could see the hunger in her eyes. The need to hear about her brother, lost so young.

"He was hell on wheels when we were out of pocket. It didn't matter where we were. D.C. or Kenya or Panama. He'd own the room before we left, and leave them wanting."

She bit her lower lip, and he wasn't sure if it was to stop from laughing or crying.

"I can't tell you how many times he'd fall back into his cot at three in the morning, totally AWOL, drunker than shit, then get up an hour later and outrun the whole team on the obstacle course. I still don't know how he did it."

"God, he was just like that at home. Not the drinking part, he was too young, but he was always sneaking out of the house, and he never got caught. I ditch one day of school, and I'm on restriction for life."

"Sounds right." He drank some coffee, more for the distance than the taste. He wasn't here to get nostalgic and emotional. In fact, the last thing he needed was to care about anything but the job. He'd need to be on his game, and there was nothing that screwed up a man faster than letting his defenses down. "He talked about you."

"Yeah?"

Boone nodded. "He worried about you. But he was proud. Real proud."

She turned to look at Milo for a long minute. The dog wagged his tail at the attention, then came to her for a pet. "He was a great brother, until a couple of years ago. Then, I don't know." She looked at Boone again. "He changed.

He got paranoid, and he hardly ever called. When he did, he wouldn't tell me squat. Just that he was in the middle of something. I only saw him the one time—"

She stood up and put her mug in the microwave. "What were you guys doing in Kosovo?"

"I can't tell you that."

"Great. That's just perfect. And I'm supposed to trust you with my life?"

"Yeah, you are. And I'd hope you'd realize that my silence, Nate's silence, was for your protection."

"Spy central. Jesus. Don't you know your big-boy games can get people killed?"

"Yeah. I know. But that's not the issue now. What's on the table is the stalker and how we're going to stop him."

"Wait." The microwave dinged and she came back to the table with the steaming coffee. "I'm not finished with the question portion. What's with the pizza parlor?"

Boone bit back his impatience. She was scared, she didn't know him from Adam and he needed to make her trust him. "It's got a special phone. One that monitors calls from the old team. Just in case."

"In case what?"

"Things didn't exactly end for any of us. Not for Nate, not for me. We needed a way to communicate with each other that wouldn't get us noticed. So we have Gino's."

"Didn't end? You mean something bad went down in Kosovo, don't you? Something that shouldn't have happened. And someone isn't happy about it, right? That's why Nate left the service. That's why he was killed."

Boone nodded.

"Great. Are the feds going to bust in here and arrest us both? Because, while it would solve the stalker problem, it doesn't seem like the best possible outcome."

"Now I really know you're Nate's sister. Don't worry. No one knows I'm here. No one's going to. And while this has been fascinating, we have work to do."

"What kind of work?"

He leaned forward, glad the Q & A was over, although a little surprised she hadn't pressed for more. "I've written an e-mail I want you to send. The geek installed key-logging software on your computer, and I want to use that."

"Wait, what?"

"Do you know what key-logging is?"

"Yeah. It's for wives who want to spy on their husbands."

"And for stalkers who want to spy on their victims."

She closed her eyes and took a deep breath. When she opened them again, her brown eyes were serious and determined. "Fine. Whatever it takes. I want him taken out."

"Can you use that gun of yours?"

"Well enough."

"You hadn't released the safety. When you came to shoot me in the hall."

"Oh."

"Can you defend yourself, hand-to-hand?"

She lifted that right eyebrow of hers, and he had to admit, even with all that had gone down with her, she was still a great-looking woman. Too bad this was work.

"You will." He stood up, took his cup to the sink and rinsed it out. "I want to do that e-mail, then we're going

to the store. From today on, you eat, and you eat well."
He turned and gave her his no-excuses glare. "You'll
sleep, too. But mostly, you're going to do everything I
say. Got it?"

TOUCHING THE COMPUTER WASN'T easy. Just knowing
he'd been there. That he'd been monitoring every single
keystroke. Looking at the sites she'd visited, checking
out her Google searches. It made her skin crawl.

It helped that Boone was right next to her, although
that wasn't all peaches and cream, either. Yeah, she
needed the help, but doing everything he said? That
was a bit much.

Then again, her options were pretty damn narrow.
"Okay, who do I send it to?"

He gave her an address that seemed ordinary enough.
And he scooted his chair closer. So close, his thigh
brushed against the side of her butt. In a move both un-
characteristic and slightly humiliating, she felt her
cheeks fill with heat. She concentrated on the typing.

"Ready?" he asked.

She nodded.

"Hi, Gina," he said, waiting for her to type the words.
"Guess who's back? Boone is here and he's going to
take care of everything. That problem I told you about
is going to be resolved soon. Anyway, don't worry, it's
under control. I'll call you as soon as things are back to
normal here. Take care, Christie."

She finished it up, then waited for the word to hit Send.

Boone nodded, and she hit the key, knowing the
bastard was reading about his own demise.

"Why are we sending this?" she asked.

"To get him to move in."

"Uh…"

"We can't do anything if he stays in the background. He already knows his bugs have been detected, so he's suspicious. Today, I'm going to make sure he knows we're a couple. In fact, we're going to do that right now. You ready to go to the store?"

"Together?"

"Yep."

"Let me get my purse."

"Skip it," he said, as he pushed his chair back. "It's all part of the service."

Christie thought about protesting, but Boone knew the situation with her finances. She'd just have to make sure and write down how much he spent so she could pay him back. Every penny.

They stood at the same time, moving into the same space. She bumped into his chest. His hands gripped her shoulders, and she froze. Her head tilted back to look up into his face, and when she found him staring at her with his ocean eyes, she shivered.

The seconds slowed while her heartbeat sped. She'd been terrified in his arms last night, but now his size, his hardness, gave her strength. But that wasn't what made her pulse race. It was the way he looked at her. Like a predator. Like a man who wouldn't stop until he got what he wanted. And it felt an awful lot like he wanted her.

He dropped his hands, and before she could even blink he was out of the office, his heavy footsteps loud in the hallway.

It took her another minute to get her act together, to realize how ridiculous she was being. He didn't want her, for God's sake. They'd met twenty seconds ago. He was here as a favor to her brother, a debt to be paid. She was a walking wreck who could barely string two coherent thoughts together.

She followed him down the hallway, dismissing her temporary insanity. This wasn't her life. It wouldn't be her life again until the bastard was behind bars. Nothing mattered but that. Nothing.

HE TOOK HER OUTSIDE, WALKING slowly past the hidden camera that was just below the eaves of her roof. There was no way this exit would be missed. That, in combination with the e-mail, should shake things up. Boone just hoped he could prepare Christie for what was to come. He would be right with her, but that wasn't enough. She was going to have to learn to defend herself. Later, he'd take her to the gym, and he'd show her some moves. Tonight, he'd take her to the shooting range. By the time he was finished with her she might not be a sniper, but she'd know enough to hit her target and not herself.

"Slower," he whispered, careful not to move his mouth much. He slipped his arm around her shoulder and felt her tense. But he smiled, stepped closer to her, wanting the geek to assume they were a couple. Jealousy was one of the triggers that would make a stalker act. That's exactly what Boone wanted.

They strolled down her walkway toward his Explorer. He'd parked it across the street, a few doors down, and while he knew the camera was above the eaves, he didn't know the range, so they'd keep it up until they cleared the block.

It wasn't a hardship. Damn, she smelled good. He didn't think she wore any perfume, which was just what he liked. He pulled her closer, wanting more of the sweet scent, then leaned close to her hair.

A hint of citrus made him run his hand up her shoulder to the first curve of her neck. Soft skin that even his calloused fingers could appreciate stirred more than his interest. It had been a long time since he'd been close to a woman. There was no way he could, not safely, which was just another reason he wanted the get the pricks who'd put him in this position. There was a time he'd thought about having a wife, a family. Now, the best he could hope for was a few stolen hours with a willing stranger.

Today, at least, he could enjoy the feel of her, the way his hip pressed into the curve of hers. He could even toy with the idea of more…at least until they got to the car.

"You okay?" he whispered.

"No. I'm most definitely not okay," she said. "He's watching, isn't he?"

"Yes."

"You want him to think we're lovers."

"Yep."

"So he'll come after me."

They got to the sidewalk, and he stopped her there. If the camera was on them, the geek would only see their backs. "Listen to me. The sooner he makes his move, the sooner he's out of your life. He may be coming after you, but he'll be getting me. Trust me. He's gonna be damn sorry he was ever born."

She turned and he saw her eyes were glistening. Her hand came up slowly and she touched his cheek with two fingers. She didn't linger, letting her hand fall to her side. "Boone?"

"Yeah?"

"Take the bastard down. So far down he'll never see daylight again."

"You got it."

"Promise?"

"Cross my heart."

She smiled.

He leaned in and kissed her. If pressed, he'd swear it was for the camera, but he'd be lying. He wanted to kiss her, to taste her. But he'd keep it easy. No sense freaking her out any more than she already was. He just held her loosely and enjoyed her soft lips.

As he pulled back, her hands tightened on his shoulder, and damned if she didn't part those lips and slip him the tongue. No fool, he went with the flow, and right then, that very second, a whole world of possibilities blossomed.

4

HE WAITED AS THE PICTURE emerged from the printer, and leaned back in his leather chair, his attention divided between the monitor and the photo. They were leaving the house, which gave him a window of opportunity. The problem was what to do with it?

The photo came out, a very clear picture of the man she called Boone. An ex-lover? He didn't think so. He'd never come across the name, not in any of his research. So who was he, and how come he knew how to look for the cameras?

There was a simple way to find out. He took the picture and put it facedown on the fax. He hit speed dial One, and there it went, off to his friends who would find out everything there was to know about Big Boy Boone.

It didn't matter. His plan was still in motion, on course. Soon, she'd be ready for him. Soon, she'd see that there were no other options. That there was no place to run, no way to hide. Boone, whoever he was, could be used to that end. He smiled, thinking of the possibilities.

"BOONE, WOULD YOU JUST STOP?" Christie planted her feet in the breakfast food aisle. "Hey, I'm talking to you."

He turned his head as he continued walking. "Then you'd better catch up."

She thought about walking out of the store. But she didn't even have enough cash to get home. He'd taken her a long way from Culver City to a humongous Costco, where he'd gotten a huge cart, and without even asking her, had started filling the damn thing. Her anger mounted as she followed him. "It's my damn house," she said, "and I don't like that kind of paper towel."

Boone looked at her with infuriatingly calm eyes. "Look, let's just get this over with. We have a lot to do today, and shopping isn't the priority."

"Then let *me* shop."

He turned back to the granola. "It's fuel, Christie. It's paper. It's soap."

"It's my house."

He looked at his watch. "Twenty minutes, we're out of here."

"Fine." She walked past him as he dumped a box of Grape Nuts in the cart. She got her Lucky Charms and dared him to say one word. He didn't. But he didn't stop. He just kept putting things into the cart, without asking. Well, two could play that game.

She got a giant-sized box of Twinkies and put them in the cart.

Boone snorted, but he didn't say anything.

He turned to the next aisle, and she followed, getting more pissed by the minute. He didn't even glance at her when she put in the giant tub of the highest-fat ice cream in the place.

By the time they got to the checkout, the cart was filled to capacity. Christie couldn't believe the amount of vegetables and fruits. Did he ask her if she liked eggplant? No. And what the hell was with all the Brussels sprouts? She wasn't eating them, not if he begged her.

"Are you done?"

"Does it matter?"

"Christie, we have—"

"I know. Things to do. It's only food. It's only paper."

Boone left the cart in the checkout line and came right up to her, right into her space. "What are you doing?"

She put her hand on the pastry counter. "I'm going to get a cheesecake."

"A cheesecake."

"That's right."

He closed his eyes, and she watched the muscles in his jaw flex. When he looked at her again, his green eyes looked cold as ice. "Is that really necessary."

"Yes. Cheesecake is always necessary."

"Goddammit, do you want this asshole to kill you? Is that it?"

She stepped back, the bluntness of his words more shocking than the bitter tone.

"Miss, you okay?"

Christie blinked at the store clerk, a skinny blonde with a problem complexion. She wanted to warn him away, but Boone turned on him first.

Not a word was spoken. She couldn't see Boone, but she didn't need to. The terrified expression on the clerk's face said it all. He backed up into a table of minidonuts and muffins, made a choking sound, then hightailed it off to produce.

When Boone turned back, he seemed calm again. Everything except his eyes.

"All right," she said, "I'll forget about the cheesecake. But I'm not giving up my Lucky Charms."

Boone nodded once. Then he turned, and they were out of there ten minutes later.

IT TOOK THEM HALF AN HOUR to put the food away. Christie still couldn't believe how much he'd bought. She'd insisted that he give her the receipt, which was more than two hundred bucks. Despite the fact that he'd gotten all kinds of crap she'd never eat, like protein powder and bean sprouts and whole wheat bagels, she'd repay every last cent.

Being angry at someone other than the bastard was a novelty. Being away from the house and actually feeling at ease had been a revelation. Contradictory, yes, but it was completely true. She felt better than she had in so, so long, even though she couldn't shake the creeps that had hit since he'd shown her that first electronic bug.

She'd been naked. She'd gotten herself off. She'd wept, she'd ranted, she'd slept. With him watching her.

"You ready?"

Boone's voice scared her, and she jumped. "Almost."

"I'll be in the kitchen."

She turned to watch him walk down the hall. He had those long legs and damn, that ass of his. But still. He wasn't exactly Barbie's dream date. His arrogance had surprised her. Nate was like that sometimes. So sure of himself and infuriatingly cocky. Maybe it was the military that did it. Or maybe the job just attracted that kind of man.

Her fingers went up to her lips as she remembered, for the billionth time, how he'd kissed her. It was a ploy, she knew that. All for show. But it hadn't felt fake.

She still wasn't sure why she'd kissed him back like that. The easy answer was that she needed the contact. It was true, too. It had been ages since she'd touched someone else. Someone who wasn't Milo. Fear for her friends had kept her away from her usual haunts, and fear for herself had kept her wary of every man in the city. It had never occurred to her, before this horrific time, how often she was touched. A handshake. A pat on the back. A hug, a kiss, friendly or intimate, it all added up, and it was important. The lack of contact made her feel less of a person somehow. As if she weren't part of life at all.

Of course, living in terror 24/7 would do that, too. Boone could be an arrogant jerk, but under the circumstances, that arrogance was just what the doctor ordered.

She wondered if they would have to keep up the charade. If he'd kiss her again. The idea wasn't unwelcome. Oh, who was she kidding? She totally wouldn't kick him out of bed.

"Are you still standing there? You're not even dressed."

She jumped. "Relax, soldier. This isn't the barracks."

"No, it's not. It's war. And if you want to win, you'd better get that pretty ass of yours in gear."

It was hard to gripe at a guy who'd just complimented her ass. So she went with the huffy walk. That'd show him.

After she got changed into her running shorts and sports bra, she put her T-shirt back on and met him in the kitchen. He'd found her blender and he'd used it to concoct some ghastly looking goo. Which he held out to her, as if she would actually drink it. "What drugs are you taking?"

"Excuse me?"

"You must be high if you think I'm going to drink that."

He sighed heavily. "You don't even know what's in it."

"It doesn't look very good."

"It's got a lot of the stuff you need. You're weak, you're out of shape, and we have no time for screwing around. So drink it."

She took the tall glass in her hand, and sniffed. It didn't smell too horrible. And when she sipped it, she was surprised to find that it didn't taste all that bad, either. More like a fruit smoothie than ground-up spinach.

"Finish the whole thing," he said. "We need to get going."

She saluted and downed the brew. It was a lot, and by the time she'd drained the glass, he was standing at the front door, keys in his hand, waiting impatiently. He'd changed from his jeans to a pair of sweatpants and a muscle tee, which made his shoulders and arms look ridiculously buff. Damn.

"Well?"

"I'm coming, jeez."

Milo figured he was coming, too, given his hysterical bouncing by the door. Boone crouched down and scratched him behind the ears. "You want to come, boy? You want to take a ride?"

"Really?" she asked. "He can come?"

"Sure. We're going to take a run, then when we're at the gym, he can hang."

"Wow, what kind of gym lets dogs in?"

"Not the kind you're used to. Let's lock and load."

She got ready to face the camera again, while Boone got Milo's leash from the wall hook. When they went outside, Boone immediately put his arm around her shoulder. Even though it was only the second time, she focused on the reassurance, not the reason, so it was better. She leaned against him, the way she would if he'd really been her boyfriend. With Milo pulling, and Boone's hand tightening on her arm, she knew they painted a pretty picture, one that was sure to infuriate the bastard. Now, the only question was, would Boone kiss her again?

"MOVE YOUR ASS, PRATCHETT. We haven't even gone a mile."

Boone, who watched her from about a hundred yards ahead, had to laugh when the exhausted woman flipped him the bird. He knew he was pushing her. He'd trained enough in his life to know when to ease back, and they weren't there yet.

The biggest drawbacks were her sleep deprivation and the fact that she hadn't been eating, but today's workout would help with the former, and his protein shakes would start building muscle almost immediately. They couldn't afford to take it slow. She might have to protect herself tonight, tomorrow...

He kept on trotting backward, watching her run. He'd

found out she used to run a lot, and that was a good thing. Muscle memory and form were all in her favor. Now it was just a question of stamina.

But he could tell she was only going to make one mile. It was enough. Besides, they still had some maneuvers to get through at the gym, so he geared it down. "Okay, Christie. Slow her down."

She took him a little too literally, shifting to a walk, her hands on her hips, her chest heaving. Milo, who'd had himself a great run all over the grass, looked to her for a pet, but she didn't have the energy.

Boone, who hadn't even broken a sweat, moved to the two of them, wishing there were more time for him to really get in a decent run. "You did great," he said. "Got your heart pumping, just like it should."

"Right," she said, still struggling to calm her breathing. "I'll fall over dead, and then the problem is solved."

"Come on. You're doing great."

"Milo," she said, waving her hand in Boone's direction. "Kill."

Milo did come, but it was to lick Boone's hand.

"You traitor," she said.

"He knows who his friends are."

"Oh, please. You gave him a giant rawhide bone. What's not to like?"

A smart-ass answer was on the tip of his tongue, but he kept quiet. Instead, he headed toward the truck, watching the park for anyone who looked at all hinky.

He'd brought her back to his neck of the woods. He knew Pasadena. Where the restaurants were, where to get the best price for his Goldwing tires, and he knew where the dark alleys were, where a man could disappear.

He'd chosen the grassy area in front of Cal Tech, and while he saw several student types wandering around, it was mostly empty this time of day. He'd parked where he had an easy out, and despite his workout gear, he was armed.

He doubted the stalker would show in such a public place. If something was going to go down, it would be at Christie's, where the geek would have some measure of control and containment. Boone knew for a fact the geek wasn't getting into the gym.

Christie was breathing better when they got to the truck, and although Milo looked sorry to leave, he jumped into the backseat with his typical enthusiasm. Damn great dog.

Boone climbed behind the wheel, his gaze running over the length of her exposed legs. Despite her current circumstances, she still had some muscles in her calves and thighs. A few weeks with him and she'd be ready for anything. Given the time he'd allotted for this mission, he could still get her into pretty decent shape. All he had to do was keep his focus. They headed off to the gym, which wasn't far.

"I need a drink," she said, leaning her head against the side window.

"There's a water bottle in the back."

"There's a root-beer float at the Dairy Queen."

"You can have one later. After the gym."

She lifted her head to give him a dirty look. "You're not short enough to have a Napoleon complex, so, what, you used to be a drill sergeant?

"I can't believe you're bitching this much when we haven't done anything yet."

"Believe it. You don't seem to get that I haven't slept in months. How am I supposed to do all this gym crap when I can barely keep my eyes open?"

He stopped at a notoriously long red light on Colorado Boulevard. "You don't think he knows you're exhausted? That every day you don't rest, you're more vulnerable?"

She winced, then turned to face the street.

"You're going to get plenty of sleep tonight," he said. "I'll be there, and I'm not going to let anything happen to you."

Christie nodded. "I'll do my best."

"I know," he said. It would be so easy to coddle her now, to give in to those big, dark eyes. Maybe offer the kind of comfort he gave best. He just watched the traffic, front and back, making sure they weren't being followed.

After a few minutes, she reached behind his seat to get a bottle of water, her hand resting on his shoulder. The touch wasn't sexual at all. But try telling that to his dick.

THE ODOR IN THE GYM WAS a combination of testosterone and dirty socks. Christie saw one other woman inside, and she was enormous. Huge muscles, the thickest thighs and back on any woman Christie had ever seen, and a really cute hairdo. The woman was curling a barbell the size of a refrigerator, and she seemed pretty damned determined to make some portion of her body explode.

Boone didn't even blink as he led her and Milo toward a giant mat lying in an otherwise empty room. Once there, he turned, put his hands behind his back, spread his legs, and looked at her as if he were going to tell her to drop and give him twenty. Milo, the chicken, curled up by the wall, his head comfortably cradled in his paws. Christie turned to check out the quickest exit. No one was blocking her way, but there were at least four guys out there who could lift a VW without breaking a sweat, so she didn't run. Yet.

"You've never had any hand-to-hand training? Any kind of self-defense?"

"I kneed a guy in the groin once," she said. "But it wasn't on purpose."

"You remember what he did when you kneed him?"

"I believe he cupped himself and wept like a child."

"Sounds about right. Now, remember what you did to me when I had you?"

She nodded. "I hyperventilated and passed out."

He gave her an almost-grin. "Before that."

"I kicked at your leg, and hit you with the back of my head."

"Exactly. The head butt was a good move, one that could have worked, at least in part. But kicking my leg with your bare feet wasn't very effective."

"Milo was supposed to attack."

"You can't depend on Milo or me. For the purposes of this lesson, you're on your own, and this guy means business."

The reassurance she'd felt being with Boone all morning fell away as her situation came home once more. She wasn't safe, not even a little. And this might just be the most important lesson she'd ever learn. "All right. Tell me what to do."

From his parade-rest position, Boone looked past her and nodded. She turned to find a hulk of a man encased in rubber so thick he couldn't put his arms down. He wore a football helmet and huge handguards. She doubted he'd feel a cannonball hit at fifty feet.

"This is Josh," Boone said. "You cannot hurt him, but I want you to try."

"Okay. How?"

"Come behind me and try to choke me."

"I thought Josh and I were going to mix it up?"

"You will. But not for a while. He has somewhere to be." Boone turned toward the man. "One hour." Then he faced her again. "Okay. Take me out."

She walked around to Boone's back, feeling the flex of the mat underneath her sneakers. Not sure if she was supposed to try and surprise him, or strangle him, or just put her arm around his neck, she went for the full court press. The second she had her arm in place, it was swept away, she was spun around, and her arm was pulled uncomfortably high up behind her own back. That was only the beginning.

Boone made her try every kind of attack she could imagine. From the front, from the side, from the top as if he were sleeping, when he was walking, when he was running. And he defeated her with such ease tears came to her eyes. Not because she was hurt, although she was sore, but because her own uselessness hit her harder than he ever could.

What hit her equally hard was that she hadn't just missed being touched, she'd been starved for it. Every block, every hold, and even though she was fighting as hard as she knew how, she was completely aware of all the body parts and where they met.

He actually flipped her over, and to keep her completely immobilized, he lay on top of her, flat out, breast to chest. For a long minute, she stared into green eyes that seemed lit by an inner fire. The next minute, with his breath and her breath swirling between them, she thought sure he was going to close the distance and kiss her. But he blinked.

The next thing she knew, he was on his feet and out of the room.

She stared at the ceiling as she tried to calm the hell down. This was war. He'd been very specific. And in war, there was no room for the sex.

Boone walked back in. She felt his footsteps on the mat, felt his presence as he approached. He didn't come too close. Instead, he told her, in his most military voice, to get to her feet. It was time for her to start the active phase of today's lesson.

"*Start* the active phase? What the hell have I been doing for the last hour?"

"Learning, I hope."

Behind him, Josh reentered the room, still wearing the puffy suit. Boone moved aside and didn't say anything more. He just waited and watched as Josh attacked.

The first time she hit back it was so girly it made her blush. An hour later, she was attacking him with the weight of her body behind her, and more importantly, with the strength of Boone's conviction that she had all the resources she needed to win.

By the time he called it quits, she was dripping with sweat, shaking from exhaustion and feeling at least a little better about her chances to survive.

She also had a brand-new appreciation for Boone, which had nothing to do with his hotness. He hadn't let her get away with squat. He didn't take any excuses and he expected her to be at her best every minute. It made her think a lot about Nate, about how he would have been right here, training her just like this, if he'd been around.

Boone finished a quiet conversation with Josh, then met her where she stood, still trying to catch her breath. He put his arm around her shoulder and leaned close. "You were awesome," he said, his voice low and intimate, but filled with conviction. "You fought like a tiger, and I feel damn sorry for anyone who tries to mess with you."

She laughed, even as the swell of pride rose up in her worn-out body. "You silver tongued devil."

"I'm not bullshitting here, kiddo. You're fierce, and don't hold back. That's gonna keep you alive."

Her ego deflated as she remembered, yet again, why she was doing all this. The bastard wasn't out of the game. "You know what's weird? I can't hold on to it. Even when it scares the crap out of me, even when I'm shaking in my boots, it won't stay in my brain. And every time I remember, it's like knowing for the first time. Knowing he's after me. That it's intensely personal, and that he's never going to just give it up."

Boone squeezed her shoulder. "You're not the victim

anymore, Christie. You're the victor. And the poor bastard doesn't even know it."

She turned her head just enough to meet his gaze. "We're gonna kick his ass."

He nodded. "We sure are."

"Cool."

"Yeah. Cool." Boone's lips parted and he moved a tiny bit closer. Her eyes fluttered shut as she waited.

5

BOONE WATCHED HER EYES close, felt her breath as she leaned forward. His gut tightened as he moved in to kiss her, but the sound of a heavy weight just across the gym startled him into backing away.

He coughed, trying to cover his embarrassment, then turned toward Milo, who was staring at him accusingly. "Let's go. We need to grab something to eat before we go to the range."

Behind him, he heard Christie shift on the mat. She didn't say anything and he hoped she wasn't planning ways to use her new training to kick him in the nuts. She had every right. Dammit, he was the one in charge of this operation, and he'd clearly given her the wrong signals, which was not only stupid but dangerous.

He turned around to find her standing near the door, her arms crossed over her chest, her shoulders slumped. All the confidence she'd had just moments ago had vanished because he was a screwup of the first order.

"What do you want for lunch?" he asked.

"I don't care."

"Yeah, sure. Maybe we can find a diner that serves Lucky Charms."

Not a smile, not even a glance. Shit.

"Okay then, I'll take you to a place I like. It's not fancy, but it's on the way."

Christie shrugged. Then she called the dog, and when Milo approached she crouched down to give him a hug.

The woman was terrified out of her mind. She had exactly one person to turn to. "Come on. Let's hit it. I want to get in a couple of hours at the shooting range."

As she led Milo out of the gym, Boone kept a respectful distance behind her. He could tell she was sore. Her movements were stiff, her posture rigid. She'd need a long soak tonight, and an early bedtime.

He would stand guard, and he wouldn't think of anything but the job.

SHE STOOD WITH BOTH FEET flat on the floor, shoulder width apart. The headphones played no music, just blocked out sound, and the goggles hurt the backs of her ears. She stared at the target, the familiar silhouette they show in all the movies, and she imagined that it was the bastard, standing right there.

Boone had told her a gazillion things to focus on, some of them out-and-out contradictory, but she wasn't thinking of any of them. She lifted her Glock 39 with both hands, pointing it straight at the bastard's head. Between the eyes. As she squeezed the trigger, she visualized the bullet screaming from the barrel, speeding toward the sweet spot. There was still the shock of the recoil, but she'd shot the gun before, so it wasn't so bad.

She lowered her arms and whipped off the goggles and earmuffs, desperate to see the target.

"Looks good, but you shouldn't take off the goggles."

"I'm not going to be wearing goggles if he breaks into the house."

"True, but when you're here, it's important to observe all protocols."

She turned. He was still standing about a foot behind her, slightly to the right. Maybe if she looked as good as he did in goggles, she'd wear them, but that wasn't the point. "I want to see."

He nodded, went to the side of her booth and pressed the button. Just like on TV, the silhouette man shivered as it rumbled toward her. Halfway there, she saw she'd missed the target. Completely. She sagged with disappointment. She'd been so sure.

"That's great, Christie. Good shooting."

"I didn't even hit the target."

"That's okay. Your stance was good, you were calm and you're getting better about not jerking the gun so much."

She leaned against the side of the booth, her muscles aching from calf to neck. "I can't do this, Boone. Can't we just go home?"

He shook his head and waved her into position again. His hands went to her shoulders and he leaned in, his voice low, inches from her ear. "The key in defensive shooting isn't to see how accurately you can fire a handgun, but how quickly you can fire it accurately. You need to believe you're going to hit what you aim at, every time, no exceptions. You need to be comfortable. Remember, you're going for a smooth trigger pull. Smooth and easy, nothing jerky. Be conscious of your breathing. Hold your breath, but only when you start to squeeze the trigger."

He went on, his voice even, steady, and as smooth as the breath on her neck. His hands moved down her arms, lifting them into position. She tried to listen to his advice, but she was too aware of his body pressing against hers from her shoulders to her bottom. If he hadn't shown her so very clearly that he wasn't going to go for the sex, she'd be moving back, shifting ever so slightly, just enough to get a rise out of him. Instead, she concentrated on the lesson, not the man. She just wished he smelled bad, and that his voice would stop swirling in her head.

"The only thing you should be moving is your trigger finger," he said. "Use the tip of your finger, the most sensitive spot, so you feel what you're doing. I want you to dry-fire as often as you can, get used to the feel of the weapon, make the action comfortable and easy. I want you to be so used to pulling that trigger that you don't even have to think about it."

"And just how long will that take?"

"Not long. We'll be back here tomorrow, and the next day, if we need to be."

"You said dry-fire."

"That's pulling the trigger," he said, his breath shifting just a bit so it hit her neck in a new way, "without a live round in the chamber."

"Ah. Kind of like foreplay."

He shifted back, but she moved with him. Immediately embarrassed, she pushed her hips forward, only this time, his body followed. She decided that it wasn't sexual; he was just helping her with her aim.

He cleared his throat and his grip tightened on her wrists. "Go ahead, take another shot. No headgear this time. I want you to hear the noise. Make it part of the experience."

Christie smiled. "Uh, Boone?"

Again, he cleared his throat. She didn't think it was that dry in here. "Yeah?"

"It would probably work better if the target was back in place."

His forehead hit the back of her head, a light tap, but he didn't say anything. He just let her go, went over to the side and pressed the button. The silhouette man shivered as he traveled, but once he was in place he stilled, and she wondered how she was going to convince the bastard to stand perfectly still while she remembered to breathe and squeeze her perfect shot.

Boone didn't resume his position, preferring instead to stand with his arms crossed, leaning against the partition. He watched her though, so intently the crease above his nose seemed like a dark stain.

She tried to forget about him, to incorporate all the things he'd told her about firing the gun, but it was like trying to ignore an elephant in the room. She could still feel the tickle of his breath, hear his solemn words in his dark monotone. She decided not to fight it. To let him guide her, even though he wasn't actually holding her arms.

The stance, the grip, the sight, the breath, the squeeze, and then the crack, so unlike the sounds of guns on TV, and the recoil, jolting her hands back and high.

She waited impatiently for the target to come close, and her heart did a little flip when she saw that she'd actually hit the target. Not close to the head, in fact, not even on the body itself, but there was a hole in the paper, and that seemed like an enormous victory.

"Well done," Boone said. "Good job."

She kept her cool, even though she wanted to do a little happy dance. Boone was being all business, or what she imagined all business would be for an army guy. His nod was accompanied by a frown, which she figured was Delta Force for "You go, girl."

"Let's do one more."

She nodded, wanting to keep going until she hit the body. More than the workout this afternoon, hitting the target gave her a sense of power she hadn't felt since the bastard first called. She might not be able to beat him up, but a bullet would definitely stop him.

The target took its sweet time getting back to square one, and she let Boone take her through the process as he once again watched from the sidelines.

This time, the recoil didn't seem so hard. The pull of the trigger was sweeter. But she still hadn't gotten the bullet closer to the body.

Boone took his goggles off and put them on the counter along with his headgear. He walked to her, the frown still in place, only he didn't stop a polite distance away, but got right into her face. He took the weapon from her hand, released the magazine and checked it twice to make sure it was empty, then he gave it back to her. Once she had the proper grip, he put his hand over hers and pulled the gun toward him, so the end of the barrel was right against his stomach.

"Listen up," he said, his warm breath now fanning

her lips. "If he comes and it's just you and him, forget everything you just learned. You don't aim, you don't go for balance, you don't breathe deep and hold it. You push the gun into his body." He pulled her hand, forcing the barrel deeper into his stomach. "You make contact, it doesn't matter where. Just push the gun into his body and then you pull the trigger. No finesse, no tricks. You bring him down. You don't think about it. You do it fast, you do it hard. You got that?"

She swallowed, her chest tight and hurting with the reality of what he was telling her. She might have to face a living human being and shoot him in the gut. It was something she'd never considered, not once in her life. That she would have that kind of power. That she could take that final step. But looking into Boone's steady gaze, his pupils large and dark, she knew there was no room to squirm, no room at all. If it was her versus the bastard, she had to shoot, and shoot fast.

"You got that?" he repeated.

"I got it."

He stepped back. "Let's go home."

THE RIDE HOME WAS MOSTLY silent. Boone kept a watch on the mirrors, making sure no one was tailing them, but he also kept checking with Christie. He'd done what he'd intended, hit her hard with the facts.

He'd been in the military since he joined up at twenty-four, and in the ROTC before that. His father had been a career soldier, as had his grandfather. Boone had grown up with guns, with the idea of using weapons, and he could still remember the first time he understood that he would, at some point, have to kill someone. It had hit him hard, just like it had hit Christie. Only for her, the threat was imminent.

He thought about sending her away to somewhere safer, but if she left, the geek would know and he wouldn't come out. She still wouldn't have her life back. It would mean she would be on the run for who knows how long, and he knew from experience that that kind of life sucked. Stalkers were notorious for never giving up, and this stalker, with his first-class gadgets, was no fool. The only real solution was to get him to show himself, and for Boone to take care of him once and for all.

All Boone had to do was make sure it was the geek that lost, not Christie.

Funny, though, that she'd never asked him about leaving.

"What?" she asked.

"Huh?"

"You grunted," she said. "At least I thought it was a grunt. If you burped, then I'm sorry I mentioned it."

He looked at her, at her haunted eyes. Good for her that she could keep her sense of humor. "Why haven't you asked me to help you disappear?"

She blinked a couple of times, her pretty lips parting just a bit. "Because you're going to catch him. Aren't you?"

"Yeah, I am," he said, his gaze back on the road in front of him. "We're going to."

"Don't count on me, Kemo Sabe. Despite the excellence of your tutoring, don't forget that I passed out. I'm an interior decorator. We're not known for our guerilla tactics and fighting acumen."

"You're stronger than you think. Knowing what to do is going to help. A lot."

"You catching the bastard is going to help more."

"Fair enough." He made a couple of turns he didn't need to, just as a precaution. It was no secret they were going to her place, but he didn't want any surprises. Christie was silent, but he didn't think that would last.

"Hey," she said, softly.

He turned to her, and she was staring at her hands in her lap. "What's wrong?"

"All this training, and eating right. Just how long do you think it's going to take to get this guy?"

"I don't know. We could get him tonight."

"But that's not what you expect, right?"

"There's no way for me to know. I believe the best approach is to make him jealous. To make him feel out of control, as if he's going to lose you. To me. We need to make him reckless. Our only hope is to get him so riled that he'll have to make an overt move. His goal so far has been intimidation and fear. We want him to get so furious he'd come into the house, into our territory."

"For the record, this scares the crap out of me."

"Just remember that once he steps into the house, we're in control. He doesn't stand a chance, okay? That's why we're getting you into fighting shape. We can't predict where or when he'll enter, but we can be one hundred percent ready for him. Both of us."

"So you're not going anywhere, right? You don't

have a doctor's appointment you can't miss or a date or anything?"

"No. Until we catch this guy, I'm with you. That's all."

She nodded, then leaned back, resting on the headrest. He wanted to touch her, give her some reassurance, but he didn't. Touching her had a funny way of distracting him. Even looking at her had its dangers.

As they turned the last corner, Boone slowed the truck down, searching for anything out of the ordinary. The street, typically suburban, mostly one- and two-story houses, with one apartment building on the corner, looked quiet. A lawn was being watered, and he could see the flicker of televisions through drawn blinds. The cars lining the street were ones he'd catalogued before, except for three on this side of Christie's house. He drove past it and saw two other newcomers.

One of them could belong to the geek. With a parabolic mike, he could be waiting to hear them as they walked to the front door. Boone decided to act as if that were the case. He sighed, then turned to drive around the block. "Christie."

"Yeah?"

"Just a reminder," he said, his gaze moving rapidly from the road to the assorted vehicles on either side of the street, "he might be listening."

She stiffened in her seat, and looked at him with wide eyes. "Now?" she whispered.

"No. But when we walk into the house. So we have to…"

"Act like we're lovers."

"That's right. And I want you to say something about us making it legal."

"As in getting married?"

He nodded.

After a deep breath, she asked, "What else?"

"That's it. Only, don't stop pouring it on when we get inside. I want to make sure."

"Of?"

"I want to sweep the house. For all we know, he's been there."

He could see her start to tremble. Even after she clasped her hands together. There were too many shadows to say whether she'd lost her color, but he'd bet on it. "Get your gun out of the glove compartment," he said, keeping his tone even and soft.

She did, and held it in her shaking grip.

"Load her up. Triple-check the safety, then put it in your waistband, with your T-shirt over it. Make sure you can get to it quickly."

She bent to the task as he slowed the car even further. He didn't want to turn onto her block before she was ready, physically and mentally.

He hoped, for both their sakes, that the geek would take the bait tonight. That he'd be so crazy with the turn of events that he'd let his emotions get the better of him. The angrier he was, the quicker things would end.

"Okay," she said.

He glanced over and caught her T-shirt slipping down over her jeans. He averted his gaze even though he hadn't even caught a glimpse of skin.

"There," she said, pointing to a parking spot three

houses from hers. Milo recognized home, and he got up in the back, whining to get out.

Boone parked and walked around to her side of the car to hold the door open. When she stepped out, he took her hand, and they walked together to the back to open the hatch for the dog.

Milo was quite excited and made a beeline for the front yard. Boone slipped his arm around Christie's shoulder. Her trembling was even more pronounced, although she acted the lover with conviction.

As they got closer, she put her head on his shoulder. "I can't wait to tell my mother we're engaged," she said, her voice giving nothing away. "She'll flip out."

"I look forward to meeting her. I'll call the airline tonight and make our reservations. And then you won't ever have to think of that creep again. Jesus, what a pervert. Clearly he can't get it up. If he could, he'd go after someone who wanted him."

"He's probably got one of those pencil dicks," she said. "Has to jack off with tweezers and a magnifying glass."

Boone laughed, and bent his head to kiss her. It was meant to be light, a show for the camera, if not for the microphone. But Christie...

She kissed him back. Again. Her hand went to his neck, pressing him tight, holding him as she thrust her tongue past his lips with a desperation that made him forget the microphone, the job.

She moved, pushing her body into his so that he felt the gun between them. Which meant that she would feel his erection. He couldn't stop it, couldn't will it

down. The way she kissed him after all that touching
had him as hard as the barrel.

Finally, she pulled back, but not away. She looked at
him in the dark for a long while, their breaths mingling,
her lips still moist. "I don't give a shit about that pervert," she whispered. "I just want you. Only you."

It wasn't until she stepped back, until she called for
Milo, that he remembered the words meant nothing.

THEY WALKED INTO THE HOUSE and Christie immediately went to the kitchen. Boone was still shaken from
the scene on the walkway, and as he watched her feed
Milo, all he could think was, *what the hell?*

From her career, her looks, the way her house was
so put together, he'd expected her to be...different. In
fact, Nate had told him that she was high-maintenance,
and that she had such high standards he wondered if
she'd ever meet a man who would qualify. And yet he
was absolutely sure she was coming on to him.

She put away the dog food, filled Milo's water bowl,
then turned to Boone. "I'm going to take a bath," she
said. "Care to join me?" Her voice was calm and col-
lected, but she avoided his gaze.

Was she serious? Nah, couldn't be. Was she just
reacting to the fact that the geek might be listening?

Giving him a wide berth, she left the kitchen for the
bath. All he could do was shake his head as he got his
duffel. He had a few changes of clothes in there, along
with his kit. A shower sounded like one hell of a great
idea, but first he wanted to sweep the house, make sure
no one had been inside.

He'd think about the kiss later, when they were safely settled down for the night. When they were in separate rooms. Maybe it was his problem, not hers. It had been too long, that's all. Too long since he'd been this close to someone like Christie.

SHE GOT TO HER BEDROOM DOOR and fought the urge to look back at Boone. She'd embarrassed herself enough with him for one day. She wanted him with a hunger that was foreign to her, that made her feel like a first-class slut. Ironic that for most of her adult life, she'd been considered pretty cold. She wasn't, of course. Just picky.

She went straight to the closet and turned the dimmer light on because, frankly, she didn't want to see herself in the mirror in the corner. She just stripped off the workout clothes and pulled on her bathrobe. Never so grateful for her incredible Whirlpool bathtub, she couldn't wait to get in and soak for a week or two. Anything that would make her feel like herself again. Did she even remember what that was like?

She sighed as she went to her big dresser. She got out her old pair of flannel pajamas, the ones with little cowgirls on them. They'd been a gift from her best girl-friend, Stacey, who lived, unfortunately, in Colorado. Four years ago, they'd had a slumber party, and while Christie had provided the munchies and the chick flicks, Stacey had brought matching pj's. It had been such a great night.

Christie thought about her old friend a lot, especially lately. A year ago, she'd have turned to Stacey for help, but her friend had enough on her plate. She'd married the love of her life, and they'd had a child. But the baby, a sweet little girl, was born with spina bifida. Stacey knew nothing about the stalker, nothing about the deterioration of Christie's life, and that's how it would remain. The pajamas weren't the perfect substitute for the sympathetic shoulder of a best buddy, but they'd have to do.

She slipped on her fluffy slippers, and went into the bedroom, stopping right by the bed to see if she could hear Boone. He wasn't in the shower, because she would have heard the plumbing. No, he was still going over the house for bugs. He'd probably wait until she was in the bath to do this room, which meant there was no way she was turning on the light.

She shivered as she thought about the bastard watching her, and immediately tried to think of something else. She sat on the edge of the bed and opened the bedside-table drawer. Shoving her vibrator to the very back, she pulled out one of her favorite books, something she'd read at least a dozen times, but *Pride and Prejudice* always made her feel good.

She held the book in her hand, thankful for small delights. A bath, Jane Austen, scented candles and a good night's sleep. And no thinking about Boone. Not even for a second.

Yeah, right. Clearly, she'd lost her mind, which was understandable, considering. She'd never attacked a man before, never been so brazen, so nuts. Maybe if she got a few more good nights of sleep, he wouldn't seem so attractive.

She should get up now. Go pour her bath. Maybe

she'd put that lilac-scented oil in the water, along with the Epsom salts. Thinking of the bubbles that would swirl in the tub, she stood, ready to be immersed in heat, when she brushed the back of her robe over her butt. Her hand came away damp, which was weird because Milo hadn't had an accident in a really long time, and only once on her bed when he was a puppy. She looked at her palm, but it was too dark to see. Her gaze moved to the bed. Something was wrong. Off.

She stepped back and reached over to the bedside lamp. The light spilled over the bedspread, which was stained a deep, dark, bloodred.

6

BOONE DROPPED THE SCANNER and had his weapon out before her scream died. He saw her in the room, her hands splayed to her sides, her posture rigid, her mouth open in horror. What he didn't see was the geek.

Instead of just slamming into the room, he came in soft, checking the right, the left, the windows, the closet door. Nothing. Nothing but a terrified woman standing over a blood-stained bed.

"Shit," he said, looking Christie over, even though he knew it couldn't be her blood. "Are you hurt?" He kept his voice low, although after that scream, it made no difference.

She shook her head.

"Did you see him? Was he here?"

"No."

"Go into the kitchen," he said, "and stay there."

"No. I'm not going anywhere alone."

Boone knew it wouldn't do him any good to argue with her. He moved closer to the bed. There was an extraordinary amount of blood. It had drenched the comforter, splattered the pillows and the wall behind it. Too much blood, and it didn't smell right. There was none of that copper odor he knew too well. He touched the comforter, dipping his finger in the wet, and brought it to his nose. He smelled sugar. "This is fake. It's stage blood."

"That's not as big a comfort as you'd think."

"I know," he said. "It still means he was in here, and he's probably listening, if not watching us right now."

Christie clutched her robe, but she kept her composure.

He walked to her, touched her arm. "Go into the kitchen. Take your weapon. I'll be right there."

She went into her closet and came out holding the Glock. She looked once more at the bed, at him. "I can't," she whispered.

"Okay. You stay here. Don't say anything."

She nodded. Boone doubted the camera would catch the trembles that ran through her body.

He reached for his scanner and remembered he'd left it in the other room. He looked to Christie. "I'll be right back. Stay put."

Her eyes widened, but she didn't object.

It took him a minute to retrieve the gadget, and another to get Milo from the kitchen. The dog followed him to the bedroom and immediately went to the bed to sniff the syrup. Christie called him over. Milo looked regretfully at the treat, but he obeyed and the two of them went to the corner of the room where there were no windows and hunkered down together on the carpet.

Boone's first instinct was to go over to her. She still looked incredibly scared, and her palm was smeared with the sticky red goop. He'd seen the back of her robe, which looked ruined. Just like everything else in her life. But the way he could help the most was to catch this sick freak. So he got to work.

The first camera he looked for was the one he'd placed in a hinge on the door. He didn't touch it, or even look at it, in case there were other cameras, but his meter showed him it was there and functioning. He'd look at the tape later, after Christie was asleep. The camera would have caught any activity in the room, and with luck, would identify the geek. He could then get a still, and use his buddy at the FBI to run facial-recognition software. It would be a simple matter of tracking the stalker down once they knew who he was. Boone couldn't wait to get his hands on him. He wouldn't be stalking anyone else. Not in this lifetime.

As he went inch by inch over every surface, he thought about the significance of the blood spatter. For one thing, the geek had managed to get into the house. Boone had checked every lock, and they were damn good. He'd even jimmied a couple of them to make them stronger, but that hadn't stopped him. The fake blood was a message, but what kind? That the geek had access to her bedroom. That he wanted her dead. Or that he wanted her even more vulnerable, more frightened, now that she had someone in her corner.

He'd gone to a lot of trouble to make that quantity of goo. And he'd had to transport it here, get it inside, spread it around, all without having any idea when Christie would return home. At least, theoretically.

He couldn't have tailed them and done this at the same time. He could have an accomplice, although

Boone had never heard of any stalkers who didn't work alone. Killers, yes, but not stalkers.

What mattered was that the geek had made it into the house. That was bad. He'd scared Christie just when she was starting to get a little confidence back. That was also bad. The question now was how to make the geek do it again, only on Boone's terms.

Christie was another problem. Could he get her out, without the geek knowing? The chances of that were minimal. So they'd fight it out here, if they couldn't ID the prick. But Boone was no fool. This was a lot more complex than he'd first imagined, and he wasn't above getting help. He'd call Seth tonight, get him to take a look around.

Boone stopped. The red light was beeping, and the gadget was pointed at the edge of her blinds. He reached up and found the tiny camera, debated holding it for Seth, but decided it was too risky. He put it under his boot heel and squished it into mush.

Of course the geek knew that Boone wasn't Joe Ordinary by now. He'd known that when the first bug was smashed. It hadn't scared him off. It had spurred him on.

The geek had to be a spook. CIA, most likely, with cash to spend and incredible access, who was focusing all his energy on one woman. Why? Why her? What did he want? Was sexual obsession the whole story?

He finished the room fifteen minutes later, still with no strong theories as to how to obtain his objective. All he knew for sure was that he'd need help, and that he couldn't leave Christie alone.

He put away his scanner, and went to the corner, where Milo was taking care of Christie. Boone crouched down so he was eye level with her. "It's all clear in here now. You're okay. What do you say we get you into a bath."

She looked at Milo, rubbed him behind the ears. "I don't need a bath."

"Yeah, you do. You might need to move tomorrow. Without wincing."

She continued to pet Milo, staring at his big, brown eyes.

Boone was gonna have to shift position soon, as his leg was gonna cramp, but he didn't want to push. Tonight had given her one hell of a shock, on top of a whole lot of other shocks.

She leaned toward him slightly without lifting her gaze. "What if he can see me?"

"There are no cameras in the bathroom. I checked."

"You checked the locks. You checked the windows."

He was the one wincing, and not from his leg. "I know. I'm sorry. I underestimated him. I won't do that again."

Finally, she looked at him. "Will you come with me?"

"Oh, yeah. We'll get the bath ready together. And then I'll stand right outside the door. No one, nothing, is going to get through me, you got that?"

She sniffed, leaned over and kissed Milo on the top of the head, then she stood. It wasn't the smoothest of moves. He knew her legs, her back, her whole body had to be hurting.

He stood, his knee popping loudly, and followed her into the bathroom. It was like something out of a magazine. Not that he hadn't seen fancy baths before, but this wasn't just for show. Everything in the room was designed to pamper. The multiple showerheads, the Whirlpool tub complete with neck pillow and a wide variety of bath salts and oils. She had candles, a boom box, a dimmer switch. The towels were thick and huge, with a matching rug.

He turned on the water, made sure it wasn't going to scald her, then he looked under her sink for the Epsom salts. He found a box, and dumped a large amount into the tub.

When he stood, Christie was still standing by the door, holding the top of her robe closed with a tight fist. He got close and reached out to touch her arm, but she flinched away. Dropping his hand, he stepped back, made himself look as harmless as possible. "Soak as long as you want. I'll be right outside. I won't move, I won't need to get a glass of water. I won't make a phone call. I'll be there."

"Okay," she said, "but…"

"What? What's wrong?"

"I don't have any clothes. For after."

"What do you want? I'll go get them."

"I'll go." She stepped to the door and opened it, but she didn't walk into the hall. "Come with," she said.

He walked next to her, not touching, and kept it up until they were back in her bedroom, inside her closet. She got underwear, jeans, a T-shirt, a bra. Socks and sneakers. Then she headed for the door.

"What about pajamas?"

She shivered. "I can sleep in these."

He didn't say a word. It was smart to be prepared for anything.

They got back to the bathroom, which was warm

and steamy as the tub was almost full. He'd already made sure there were no new bugs in here, so she could soak in peace, although he doubted that would happen. "I'm going to be right outside," he said. "No one's getting past me. So don't worry about it. Take as long as you want."

She put her clothes down on the counter by the sink. For a long minute, she simply stood there, staring at her T-shirt, her back to Boone. Her hands quivered by her side.

"Christie?"

She didn't turn around. "Go on. It's fine."

He approached her softly, but he made sure she knew he was there. "Tell me what I can do," he said.

"Make it go away."

He could barely make out the words, but he heard the soft sniff. She was crying. He fought back his panic and concentrated on her, on what she needed. He'd never been able to deal with crying women. Kids, sure. Give 'em a piece of candy and they shut right up, but that didn't work so well with anyone over ten. "I will. I wish it could go faster, but trust me. He'll be gone. For now, you'll feel a lot better after a long soak in the tub."

He glanced back and saw he'd better turn off the water.

As he bent over the spigot, he felt her beside him. When he stood, she stared at him with reddened eyes, her skin so pale she looked as white as her robe.

"Stay," she whispered.

"I'm not going anywhere."

"I mean in here."

He bit his lip, not wanting to say the wrong thing. It was so quiet in the small room, not even the faucet dripped, and he wished he was someone a hell of a lot smarter. "Are you sure that won't make you uncomfortable?"

"Maybe. But I'd rather be uncomfortable than so scared I can't breathe."

He nodded, trying to understand. After looking at her hopeful gaze, he decided he didn't need to understand. He needed to do what she wanted, whatever that was. "Sure. I'll go sit over there," he said, pointing at the toilet. "You go ahead."

He went over to the toilet, put the lid down and sat, angling himself so she'd have privacy and he could see the door. His weapon was at his back, ready should he hear anything. The only thing he heard, however, was the sound of her undressing. The soft thump of her robe hitting the floor. Then there was the whoosh of her touching the water. He wasn't sure at first if it was her hand or her foot, and then it kept on going, so he knew she was naked. She was lowering her body into the tub. Getting wet. Getting warm.

His face heated as his mind pictured every inch of that body sinking into the tub. He thought about that moment at the gym, when he could have kissed her, and he wanted to shoot himself for being such an idiot.

After a deep breath, he forced himself to focus again. He was her bodyguard, not her lover. He had no business thinking what he was thinking, and he deserved the discomfort in his pants. His dick didn't know any better, but he did. Christie was his client. Clients and sex didn't mix.

"Boone?"

His name echoed slightly in that soft, whispery voice that came from fear. "Yeah?"

"Talk to me."

"About?"

"Anything. About you. Where were you born?"

He closed his eyes for a moment, clicking through the alternatives. There were several things he could tell her, and if she checked, they'd all pan out. But it felt cowardly to lie in this room, with her being so incredibly vulnerable. "Tennessee."

"I'm surprised. I don't hear the accent."

"Yeah, I had one. I got rid of it."

"Why?"

"I needed to blend in."

"Oh, okay."

He waited, unsure what she wanted from him. But then he decided she just wanted noise, something to cover the sound of her washing. "I had an older brother. Teddy."

"Had?"

"He was killed in Desert Storm."

"Oh, God. I'm sorry."

"Yeah. He was a great guy. A hell of a soldier."

"Is that why you became one?"

"No. It's just what we did. My father was a lifer. Hell, no one ever called him anything but Major. We were an army family, all the way. ROTC, enlisting the day we came of age. I never thought of doing anything else."

"What about your mother?"

He sighed. "She was a good army wife. She could pack up and move a house in a week. Nothing fazed her. She took everything like a good soldier."

"Are they still around?"

"Yeah, they are. Back in Tennessee. My father's retired. He likes to hunt now. Hunt and fish."

"Must be nice."

"What, hunting?"

"No, having parents who approve of you. Who care."

He laughed. "Boy, are you off by a mile."

The water sloshed. "But you were in Delta. That had to have made them happy."

"It did. For a while."

"What happened?"

He took in a deep breath and let it out slow. "Things didn't turn out the way any of us expected."

"You're talking about the Balkans, aren't you? About the mess that got Nate killed."

"Yeah."

He listened as she washed. At least that's what he pictured. A sponge moving over her pale skin, down her arms, dipping under the water to caress her long legs.

"Boone?"

"Yeah?"

"Do you miss your mom?"

All thoughts of wayward sponges ceased instantly with that word, but aside from the slight flash of guilt, he registered the tone of Christie's question. She was hurt, alone and in one hell of a mess. "Sometimes," he said. "Do you miss yours?"

"No," she said, her voice a lot softer than a moment ago. "I miss Beaver's mom."

"Who?"

"You know, Beaver Cleaver. His mom. She would have been great, wouldn't she? Always dressed so neat and tidy, always making sure the house was clean and dinner was on the table when Ward came home from the office. She listened to all their problems, no matter how silly they were. And she never made either of her kids feel stupid."

"Versus your mother, who did?"

"Oh, yeah. She's an expert. She loved us, I suppose, in her own dysfunctional way, but sometimes it was awfully hard to tell."

"How'd you turn out so great if she was so awful?"

She didn't answer, and he was tempted to turn and look, but he kept his focus on the doorknob, nothing else.

"Christie?"

"Just thinking," she said. "Thinking that it was my dad's influence, but it wasn't. The good parts of me are because of Nate. He wasn't that much older, but he was the adult in our house. Can you believe that? As crazy as Nate was?"

"Yeah, I can believe it. Why do you think he was the team leader? The man had some serious skills. I've never met anyone I could depend on like Nate. He was the rock, no matter what."

"Yeah. A pigheaded rock, but man, when I needed him, he was right there. You know he beat up Scott Fairchild for me? That was excellent."

"Tell me," he said, wanting nothing more than for her to relax, and for him to stop thinking about how naked she was.

"Fairchild was an ass. He was a year ahead of me in high school, and he thought he was too damn cool for the rest of us mortals. What a jerk. He used to put a chalk mark on his locker for every girl he slept with. Well, that he said he slept with. The chalk was white, and when the janitor wiped it off, he'd just chalk them up again."

"Why did Nate beat on him?"

"Because he wanted to put me on his list."

"Oh."

"No, no. It wasn't like that. It was worse. I was young and stupid and totally into wanting to be popular. So when he asked me out, I was thrilled. I spent all my babysitting money on a new outfit, and talked about it for days and days before the actual event. He picked me up, introduced himself to my parents with his Eddie Haskell manners, and the minute we were in the car, he told me we weren't going to make it to the school dance after all, but to this party at his friend's house."

"Uh-oh."

"I'll say," she said. "Of course, we were the only two at the party, and of course, he'd laid in a stash of booze. I'd known that's what he'd want, but I didn't get it. Not really. So when it came down to it, I freaked. I couldn't go through with it."

"That's good."

"Not really. Because he took me home. Dropped me off at the end of the block, not even at my house. Then he put a big old chalk mark on the locker with my initials under it. He told everyone that mattered at the school that I was not only a total skank, but that I was so lousy he was sure I was really a dyke. Nice, huh?"

"And that's when Nate showed up."

"In his uniform, thank you very much. At school. With all Scott's posse watching. Not only did Nate clean his clock, he told everyone that Scott was the most un-sophisticated, foolish little boy he'd ever seen. That a real man didn't ever need to broadcast it, that a real man had respect for women because they were the greatest of God's gifts, and that since he knew for a fact that Scott had lied about doing anything with me, it was a sure bet that he'd lied about every other chalk mark on his locker.

"Bet Scott's life was never the same again."

"Damn straight."

He angled toward her, but didn't look at anything but her eyes. "And I'll bet you wish more than anything in the world that Nate was here right now, cleaning this bastard's clock."

She opened her mouth to say something, but nothing came out. Her lips trembled and then she was crying. Eyes closed, she turned her back to him, but he could see by the way her shoulders shook that this was bad, worse than before.

He heard her sob, and all he could think was that she looked so small, so helpless in that big old tub. And how he wished Nate were there, because she needed him so badly. She needed so much.

Then he thought again about what his job was, here in this house, in this room. And he stood.

7

CHRISTIE STOPPED CRYING. Not because she didn't miss Nate, not because she'd never felt more alone in her whole life, but because she just couldn't. Her eyes couldn't weep, her throat couldn't breathe, her soul couldn't hold up, not for another second. There was nothing left in her, just numbness. A person, she supposed, could only be so scared for so long before everything shut down. It was better this way. Easier. If she just stayed in the bathtub for the rest of her life, she'd be fine. Pruney, but fine.

As for Boone, well, she appreciated that he was here. She wished she could believe that he would fix everything, but that was gone, too. Sure, he'd do what he could, but it was useless. Hopeless. Damn, if she wasn't too tired to even think about that.

She reached over and turned on the Whirlpool jets, then she leaned back so her neck was on the pillow. If she closed her eyes, maybe she could think about the water. Just the water.

It worked for a few minutes, but then she opened her eyes. She gave a start when she saw Boone right next to the tub. His legs were bare, and as her gaze moved up his body, she saw he'd taken his clothes off. He had a towel around his waist, but he was naked, all right.

"Scoot up," he said.

She heard him, but she was too confused to obey. What, all of a sudden it wasn't about the job? "What's going on?"

"Let me in, and I'll tell you."

She looked up even farther, until she met his eyes. He didn't look sneaky and he didn't leer. But she still wasn't sure.

"It's all right," he said.

She moved until her chest hit her knees. Boone dropped the towel and stepped carefully into the tub behind her, his feet touching her hips. She got as small as she could, feeling her heartbeat against her kneecaps as she waited for him to sit. He grunted as he stretched his legs on either side of her. He had to bend his knees a bit, as he was too tall, even though the tub was way oversized. Then he gave a great sigh, which she knew had to be because of the jets. His hands gripped her shoulders and he pulled her back, against his chest.

"Boone?"

"Yeah?"

"Care to share now? About what you're doing."

"Getting in the tub."

"I know that part. Why?"

"Because you're scared."

"I've been taking baths for a long time all by myself. Haven't freaked yet," she said, hoping he didn't hear the banked tears in her voice.

"You want me to get out?"

She put her hands on his knees. "No."

"Okay, then. Lean back and relax."

She did. Her head fell back to the crook of his neck, her back was cushioned by his chest and she felt surrounded by strength. The thick cock lying against her tailbone was something to think about later.

"What's the first thing you're going to do when this guy is toast?" he asked.

"Do we have to talk about him?"

"Yeah, I think we do. But it's okay," he said, as his arms wrapped around her, just above her breasts.

She felt tiny, even though she wasn't. She was five-seven, and she'd never been with any man who made her feel this delicate. Oddly, it didn't make her feel helpless. Just, small.

"I've got you," he whispered, his lips almost touching her ear.

Christie quivered, and not from fear. He had her. *He had her.* She closed her eyes, cocooned in this man, encircled by heat and flesh and wet, and she wasn't just small. She was…safe.

Her throat clenched, and it was sheer will that kept her from crying all over again. It seemed impossible that only a moment ago, she'd lost all hope, and now, with his arms, and his words, and his body, he'd changed everything.

"You okay?"

She sniffed. Nodded.

"So what's the first thing you're going to do?"

"Go to Disneyland?"

"Christie."

She smiled. He could do stern schoolmarm so well. "Get a new bed."

He chuckled and she felt it all the way down her back. "That's good. What else?"

"Get a new job, maybe? Remind my friends that I'm still alive. Take Milo to the park."

"Okay. Keep those things in mind. Keep them as close as you can. What we're going to do tonight, is get some rest. Tomorrow, we'll start again. We'll train in the morning. In the afternoon—"

"Hold it. Get some rest? I hope that means you plan to sleep with me here in this bathtub."

"Uh, no. But tell you what. I'll make us up a bed in the living room. I'll be right there, right next to you. Me and Milo. No one's getting past the two of us."

"Well, we can try."

"You'll sleep, trust me. Now," he said, releasing her from his gentle hold, "lean forward."

She did, not even questioning his motive. She curled her arms around her legs, leaned her cheek on her knee and waited.

His hands, warmed in the water, went to her shoulders. He began a massage that hurt and felt wonderful at the same time. The wonderful won hands down.

With the patience of a saint, he worked on her neck, her shoulders, even her scalp. She hadn't moaned so much since the last time she'd had great sex, and that was a long, long time ago.

He didn't do anything else. It wasn't a prelude, it wasn't about loosening her up. The thing was, they both knew he could have. That she would have welcomed a sexual touch, but that wasn't what he gave her. This was better. It was what she'd wanted even when she hadn't known how to ask.

He had her add hot water three times. Her fingers and toes looked like dried figs, but she never wanted him to stop. Those large hands, those calloused fingers, were so gentle, so amazing, she felt like a puddle of goo.

"Christie?"

"Yeah?"

"I think we'd better get out now. I'm starting to develop gills."

She smiled. Turned off the jets and lifted the plug. Her moments of peace were over. Perhaps some of these feelings would linger. If he slept close enough. If she could still feel him next to her.

Bracing his hands on the edge of the tub, Boone got out first. He got one of her towels from the rack, the big Egyptian cotton bathsheet and instead of drying himself off, he held it out for her.

All she could think as she stood, as he wrapped her in warm terrycloth, was that this might have been the kindest thing anyone had ever done for her. She wasn't used to kind men. Not good-looking kind men. That seemed to be a contradiction in terms.

The only thing she was sure of was that even though she knew the blood was still all over her bed, that the bastard had gotten into her home again, and that it wasn't over, not by a long shot, she felt relaxed. For that, the man deserved a medal.

He'd gotten himself a towel, and was using it like sandpaper. His gun, which had been right by the tub the entire time, was in his hand even before he put on his pants.

She watched the muscles ripple in his broad back, the way his bare toes tried to grip the white carpet. He turned then, and she saw that somewhere between the tub and the towel, he'd gotten hard. It was a shock to see something so sexual, to realize that he'd ignored everything but her comfort, her needs.

She walked to him, tightening her towel around her chest. When she stood directly behind him, he stopped, dead still, but he said nothing. He was bent slightly forward, his free hand flexed by his side.

Christie touched his back. His skin rippled and he sucked in a sharp breath, waiting. The only other sound was the echo of her own heart pounding in her ears. She was nervous, but sure. She wanted so badly to give him back something as intimate and generous as what he'd given to her.

With her left hand still on his back, she touched his side, being as calm and slow-moving as if she were gentling a feral cat. Her fingers slipped over the sharp curve of his hipbone, then through hair that was soft and still damp.

She found him harder now, and his gasp sharper when she touched him. First with one finger, then with two, running up his length. She curved her palm over the smooth corona—it was moist, but not from the bathwater.

Boone twitched again—his cock, and then his whole body. She could feel his tension with her left hand, his heat with her right. She didn't want to tease. She curved her hand around him and moved up and down his length, listening to his breath, feeling him in a way she'd never felt another.

It didn't take long. He'd been ready for a long time, sublimating as he tended to her fears. Now it was all focused on him, only she found herself wanting more. Selfish, she knew, but she wanted to kiss him.

She didn't. She just moved her hand faster, pumping his flesh, waiting until every muscle in his body tensed, his head jerked back, his legs shook.

His hand went to her wrist, stilling her.

"It's all right," she whispered at the shell of his ear. "I've got you."

He let go.

When he came, it was quiet. Banked so tightly, she wondered if it physically hurt him. She continued to move her hand, but far more gently now. Releasing him wasn't easy. She walked to the second sink, washed her hands then dampened a washcloth. She handed it to him. He didn't say anything, or even look at her.

Feeling suddenly shy, she turned her back to him while she dressed. It felt weird to put on her jeans, but she wasn't taking any chances.

When she turned around again, he was in everything but his shoes. "Boone?"

Finally, he looked at her. Straight on. With his elegant green eyes and his dark, thick lashes. "Yeah?" he asked.

"Thanks."

He breathed in and out, his nostrils flaring slightly. Then he gave her that half smile of his. "We're a team."

She smiled back. "You bet."

"I'm gonna do another quick check of the house. You want to come, or stay in here?"

"Come."

"Let's lock and load."

HE WATCHED THEM, WISHING he could move the cameras so he could see her better. She was losing it. The blood had been a stroke of genius. And when he killed Boone in front of her eyes? That would be the crowning moment of his plan. She'd be his, then. And she'd do exactly as she was told.

THEY MOVED THE MATTRESS FROM the guest bed to the floor of the living room. Christie never left his side. When he went to the kitchen, there she was. When he ran his equipment around the front door, she stood patiently waiting, even though he knew she had to be exhausted. The physiological comedown from the shock of finding the blood would drain her of energy. Add to that the bath and the massage, and she should be out cold.

He was counting on that. He needed to look at his video, and he didn't want to wait until morning. If there were any chance of identifying this asshole, he wanted it now.

He had to keep pulling himself back to the job, ignoring what had happened in the bathroom. It didn't mean anything. She'd given him comfort, just as he'd given that to her. And it was done. Over.

The house checked out, although Boone didn't have the same confidence in his equipment after the break-in. He just kept things low and slow, and if the geek was watching, he wouldn't see anything Boone didn't want him to see.

Unless there was some kind of camera Boone couldn't detect in the bathroom. But then, even if it did give him the major wiggins, if the geek had watched them in there, so much the better. It would inflame him to make a move, to make a mistake. Which was not something he was going to share with Christie.

She finished putting the covers on the mattress while he got out a flashlight and set it where she could find it easily in the dark. Everything was done. All that was left was bed.

Jesus, it had been unbelievable with just her hand. What would it be like to have it all? To take what he really wanted?

No, no. *Hold it, soldier.* He'd gone into that bathtub to give her what she needed. Safety. Comfort. Relaxation. It hadn't been about sex. He hadn't even touched her in any sensitive areas.

He wasn't used to this. Where he traveled, the way he lived, there was no safety. Very little comfort. And relaxation usually came after a lot more alcohol than he cared to admit. But he was responsible for this woman. For keeping her alive and well.

She made it awfully tempting, though. Even with her skinny legs and her tiny little wrists, she got to him. It hurt, how badly he wanted to squash that bug of a geek who was after her. In order to do that, he had to keep his eye on the prize. He had to get her ready, make her an ally, not a liability. He had to incite the geek to rage, to make him come into the trap. And he had to make sure he was on task 24/7.

Unfortunately, the way to get the geek into position was going to seriously test Boone's ability to stay focused.

"Hey, you okay?"

Boone blinked. Christie was standing by the bed, hands on her hips, hair all over the place. He smiled, but only for a second. "Let's get some sleep."

"You're one weird dude, you know that?"

"It's been mentioned."

"So that's it? We just go to sleep?"

"Best thing we can do," he said as he stood up, to the dismay of Milo. "We need to be sharp. All in."

"Well, for that, I'd need to have a month in Tahiti— is that on your agenda?"

"Sorry, wish I could help."

She sighed. Looked down at her feet. "Ever slept in your boots, Boone?"

"More times than I can count."

"I guess sneakers shouldn't be a problem, huh?"

"I think you'll be okay without them. Just leave them untied and ready to go."

"Nah. If they keep me awake, I'll reconsider."

"Sounds good. Now climb in."

She looked around her house, then at Milo. "Come on, boy. You get shotgun. Pardon the pun."

Milo walked around the bed, delicately sidestepping the overhanging covers. He turned in two circles, then curled into a ball, watching Christie with clear, clever eyes.

Christie pushed back the covers and climbed in. She pulled them up her neck, but Boone could see her discomfort, even underneath the blankets. He didn't blame her, but he hoped her exhaustion would take precedence over her fear. The only thing he could give her now was a body and a weapon at the ready. He slipped off his shoes, and he moved in next to her.

She faced Milo. Boone faced the front door. He could hear her breathing, could feel her tension. Milo licked some part of his body for longer than seemed necessary, and then, after a soft chuff, fell silent. Boone went through the scene again. Not the one in the bathroom. The one in her bedroom.

He went step-by-step through each move the geek would have taken to make it happen. He thought about where he'd put the camera and where he'd put the microphones. Boone knew without a doubt that there would be no fingerprints, no trace evidence at all. The fake blood was easy to make from common ingredients found in any supermarket. Even if the geek jerked off, which he probably had, he'd have been careful about that, too. No evidence. Nothing for the police.

But this asshole didn't fear the police. He didn't fear anything. Because he knew more than the cops. He was a spook, a ghost, someone who'd been into the trade-craft long enough to learn the tricks and the traps. But he was unstable, a stalker. Which probably meant he was an ex-spook.

How had he met Christie? At a party? A bar? She may have smiled at him once, in passing. Sometimes that's all it took for a stalker to become obsessed. Or maybe it had been more. A date, several dates.

Nate had said she was picky, that she didn't suffer fools. She'd probably dated the geek, didn't like what she saw, and she'd kicked him to the curb.

Christie shifted, and he stopped breathing so he could listen. He had no idea how much time had passed since they'd laid down, but it was evidently long enough for her to find sleep. He closed his eyes for a moment, just feeling her body heat. They weren't touching. The mattress was a king, which gave them some room. He wished it were a twin.

No, he didn't. If they'd been forced together it would have made it much more difficult for him to climb out without waking her. He would wait until she had a chance to get into REM sleep, when it would be most difficult to wake her. That was approximately forty-five minutes.

As the minutes ticked by, it wasn't the geek he thought about. Not the tape he was going to view. It was Christie's hand. The feel of her skin. How her muscles had relaxed underneath his steady pressure. Her hair had been swept up with some kind of wooden pin, and he'd stared at it for a long time, trying to figure out exactly how it worked. It didn't matter. the important thing was that he could see her neck so clearly. It was a lovely, slim neck. Long, delicate. Her shoulders were small, too. Such a small person.

Women in general knocked him out, but touching her had made him feel so goddamn protective. He'd never tell her that, though. She needed to feel strong. Powerful.

The geek wouldn't get within ten feet of her, but still, she deserved to feel sure that she could take care of herself. That no man, no maniac, could take her against her will.

It would take a lot more training than he'd be able to give her. But he'd encourage her to continue once he was gone. To give herself that gift.

He listened again, her soft breath coming easily, steadily. It was still too soon. And she was too close.

Christ, why had he gotten into that tub with her? He'd thought it would help. That it would make things easier. He was a moron.

Somehow, he made it through until he felt sure she wouldn't rouse. He got out of the bed as stealthily as if he were walking into enemy territory, and had a target painted on his back. Milo wasn't impressed.

The two of them went into the bathroom, with a quick stop first to pick up his equipment bag. Once there, Boone sat on the toilet again, seat down, light dim. He pulled out a portable VCR that ran on batteries. Then he put the tape in.

The camera was motion-triggered. But the first motion on the tape wasn't the geek. It was Christie. And she was in her bra and panties.

Boone fast-forwarded. The light went off, and the light stayed off, but that was okay, because the camera had infrared. It wouldn't give Boone a clear picture of the man, but it would give him a lot of intel. How big, what build, what equipment, how he was dressed, how he got in. And out.

And, like magic, there he was.

8

CHRISTIE WOKE when she kicked him. Boone didn't move an inch. She had no idea what time it was. Not too early, because the sun streaming through her living room blinds was strong. Milo snuffled, then rose, walking toward the kitchen without a backward glance. She stared at Boone.

He was such a puzzle of a man. Nothing like Nate. At least not where women were concerned. She had no illusions about her late brother. He'd been born a hound dog and he'd died one. If there was a woman within a fifty-mile radius, he knew about it, and he didn't let man or war get in the way. Not that the women had complained. Christie felt sure every one of them had fond memories of their brief stints with Nate. She also felt sure that wherever he was, he was smiling and remembering each and every one.

Which was exactly what she'd expected of Boone. They were buddies, pals, and they did their secret work in secret places together, side by side. Surely they'd whored together, too.

She watched his eyes move behind his lids. What was he dreaming about? Some mission in Panama? Or the Balkans? Or Iraq? Or was it one of his other conquests?

She liked his face. Oddly, his nose was on the small side, but it worked. His lips, now they were something. And man, did he know how to use them.

As if he'd heard her thoughts, his lips parted and she glimpsed his teeth, so straight she knew he'd had braces as a boy. Her gaze moved back to his eyes. Still darting about. And his lashes. Geez, they were long. She'd love lashes like that. They fanned out in perfect arcs, and when they were standing outside in the sun, they cast perfect little shadows above his cheeks.

Altogether a very doable guy. Who had slept next to her all night without even the slightest nudge. Weird.

Milo whined from the kitchen, and Christie climbed off the mattress as carefully as she could. Despite what lay behind her bedroom door, she wasn't nearly as scared now, not in the light. So she went to feed her dog, give him fresh water and start the coffee.

He'd been feeding her. Boone, not Milo. Feeding her vegetables and fruits and blender concoctions and pasta. He was obsessed with health, and all she could think of was chocolate. Not just any chocolate, but Godiva chocolate, in the little gold box. Well, boxes. As many as she could hold. But of course, with all the training and all the shooting, and all the blood all over her bed, there wasn't time to go to the mall. Yeah, she had the Twinkies, but it wasn't the same.

She shivered as she dished out Milo's breakfast. He went immediately to the task while she turned her attention to the coffee. Nothing could be done before she'd had at least two cups.

Once the coffee was brewing, she headed to the

bathroom. When she got out, there was Boone, standing in the hallway, his gun present and at the ready.

"Dammit, Christie," he said, lowering the weapon. "Why didn't you wake me?"

"You were dreaming. It seemed a shame to interrupt."

"Dreaming? Are you nuts?"

"I'm pretty sure I am, yes."

"Okay, then," he said, wiping his right eye. "Is the coffee ready?"

"A couple of minutes."

He nodded, then took her place in the bathroom.

She stood for a moment, watching the door. Then she turned, headed for the kitchen just in time to see Milo slip outside via the doggy door.

She wanted to change clothes. She didn't care into what, just something she hadn't slept in. But that would mean going in her bedroom, and she wasn't up to that at all.

Yeah, she was a miserable shot, but if she could get him in her sights, oh, man, she knew she'd hit a bull's-eye. Several times.

As she reached for her big mug, the one with the purple glaze, something caught her eye out the kitchen window. A truck, old and dark, pulling up to the curb in front of her house.

In an instant, she was trembling. Her heart pounded so hard in her chest she could hardly breathe. She tried to convince herself that it wasn't anything to do with her. Why should it be? This was a public street in the middle of Culver City, but oh, crap, why right there?

She backed up as the truck door opened. A woman stepped out. She was dressed in jeans and a blue sweater, and had a big canvas bag over her shoulder. Behind her, a man walked around the front of the truck. He was tall, big, like Boone. He carried a duffel bag with him that weighed a lot. He, too, was in jeans, but damn if she couldn't imagine him in a uniform.

"Boone?" she called, shouting toward the hallway. "Are you expecting visitors?"

He didn't answer, but her heart calmed down as she remembered him mentioning a friend he needed to call. She was glad she'd made a big pot of coffee. And curious about the woman.

Boone walked into the kitchen and headed for the coffee.

Christie nodded at the window. "Friends of yours?"

"Yeah," he said, making a 180, so he could meet them at the front door.

She followed. The couple walked in without talking. Both the woman and the man shook his hand, as if they were business associates.

Boone closed the door, locked it, then turned to Christie. "Seth, Kate, this is Christie."

They nodded at her solemnly, then turned to Boone. "Where do you want me to start?" Seth asked.

He was actually taller than Boone by a couple of inches, and he had eyes to die for. What was it about Delta Force that brought them such gorgeous men?

"Bedroom," Boone said, nodding down the hallway.

Seth shifted his duffel to his other hand and headed away.

"Do you want some coffee?" Christie asked, as he passed.

"No, thanks."

"What about me?"

It was the woman. Kate. Christie faced her, and saw that she was attractive, in a hard kind of way. Stark lines, great cheekbones, but cold, too. Even her voice was hard. Although she had amazing hair. Dark, long, straight and so shiny it looked as if she could have been in a shampoo commercial.

"I'm going to work with Seth," Boone said. "You two have some coffee. Talk."

With that cryptic assignment, Boone went right to the bedroom, leaving Christie with this rather dour, strange woman.

When Christie faced her, Kate didn't seem at all disconcerted. "You have real cream?"

Christie nodded. "This way."

BOONE WAS CROUCHED DOWN beside Seth's duffel, checking out the neat toys. "How do you get this stuff?" he asked.

"I have my ways."

Boone knew he'd never get more information than that. He glanced at the bed beside them. The fake blood had turned a deep, viscous brown, and smelled sickly sweet. But he wasn't thinking about the bed. "This asshole's about six feet tall, slim, he wore goggles. He didn't turn on the lights. The blood was in a big container—plastic, I think—and he was in and out in seven minutes. It was highly polished for a passion stalker."

"Who says it's passion?"

"What else?"

"Lots of things. Revenge. Money. Sex."

Boone sighed as he stood. "I thought about all of that, but blood on the bed? That's spells passion to me. I don't know. Maybe Kate can figure it out."

"Don't count on it. Hey, what's this?" Seth moved to the bedside table, and slid the whole unit out from the wall. He looked under the lip, ran his hand down the wood, then stopped. It took him a second, but he pulled out a strip of dark tape.

"What's that?"

Seth held up his other hand, then took a magnet from his bag and ran it over the tape four or five times. "It's a new kind of bug. It records audio data, but it's very sensitive. I just scrambled it but good."

"Shit, where's he getting this stuff?"

"He obviously has deep pockets."

"Yeah. That's what I was thinking."

"CIA, maybe?"

"More likely than FBI."

Seth sat back on his haunches and looked at Boone. "We shouldn't be messing with this. Maybe this isn't just about Christie. You know that, right?"

"Nate's dead, Seth. Everything he knew went with him."

"We know that."

Boone dragged a hand through his hair. "So do they. I can't think of one reason they'd go after Christie. She's completely on the outside."

"I hope you're right. It's our lives, bro."

Boone stared at his friend for a long time. "There's only one way to know for sure. We catch him."

"Let's hope he's the only one who gets caught."

CHRISTIE SAT ACROSS THE TABLE from Kate, who sipped her coffee and looked at Christie as if she were going to have to draw her face from memory. "So, uh, how do you know Boone?"

"We hang out at the same places. Know some of the same people."

"Were you in the service?"

Kate shook her head. "I worked for the UN"

Christie waited, but it was clear Kate wasn't going to elaborate "What do you do now?"

"I work for an R & D firm in Canoga Park."

"I see," Christie said, even though she didn't. Was everyone in Boone's life so secretive? Jeez, it was like living in a spy novel. "What is it you're supposed to talk to me about?"

Kate smiled. It was a nicer smile than Christie expected, and there was some real warmth behind it. "Men."

"In general?"

"No. Men you know. Or have known. We need to find this creep, and the odds are, you've either met him, or had some kind of relationship with him."

"You don't think I've wracked my brain trying to figure this out?"

"The point is, you've wracked your brain. Now it's my turn."

"You're not thinking of using needles, right?"

She laughed. "No. Sodium pentathol is so Cold War. We're just going to talk."

"That's a relief."

"Then if we don't find anything, I have drugs."

Christie looked at her for a long while before she got that it was a joke. "This is my first cup of coffee. Don't mess with me until at least cup three."

"Check." Kate reached into her big bag and pulled out a notebook and a pen. "Let's start from the beginning. Any boyfriends in high school?"

"You're not serious."

"As a heart attack."

"Okay then." Christie sipped her coffee as she went back to high school. It hadn't been a good time for her. She'd gotten good grades, but had to work hard for them. She'd also been on the track team and tried out for cheerleader. She hadn't made it. Then there was that whole Scott Fairchild incident. "In my senior year I went out with a guy named Jim Lynsky."

"Tell me about him."

"He transferred into my high school that final year. He'd come from Yugoslavia, of all things. His father was a doctor there."

"Really?" Kate jotted down notes, and she was very fast. Her writing was neat, tiny and from what Christie could see, fastidious.

"We only went out for about four months. He was into surfing and when he figured out he could get somebody better than me, he did."

"Ouch."

"I've had better days."

"Okay, college."

He sat staring at the monitor, even though it had no image. Big Bad Boone had done a good job of cleaning out the house. Not perfect, but good.

He closed his eyes, remembering her scream. The sound of it had given him an incredible erection, and he was tempted to play the tape again. But there were things to do. Lots of interesting things. The anticipation was almost as good as the scream. Especially now that he knew all about lover boy.

SETH HAD FOUND FOUR MORE strips of the bug tape, the most disturbing one under the box spring. While he worked, Boone stripped the bed and cleaned up all traces of the sticky blood. He found fresh sheets in the hall closet to remake the bed, although he doubted Christie would be sleeping there any time soon. At least it didn't look like a set piece from *Friday the 13th.*

Seth also took a look at the camera Boone had set up, and he made a few adjustments. They put a second camera in the closet, and a third focused on the window. They could see exactly how the geek had gotten access to the house; he'd cut the glass all around the outside edge, then when he was through, he'd put it back so it was virtually undetectable. Seth had glued the pane in place and added a nifty little trip wire that would alert them to any future attempts.

"I think this room is good," Seth said. "What next?"

"The kitchen, then the living room. We'll do the guest room last."

"What about the bathroom?"

"You can scan in there, but no cameras."

"Is there access?"

"Yeah. Change all the locks. And there's the garage and her car."

"Got it. You know I could use some of that coffee now."

Boone went to the door. "You still like it black?"

"Yup."

Boone left him and headed for the kitchen. He slowed as he approached, standing just within earshot of the two women.

"That's Dan Paterson. He's a psychologist. He was nice, when I needed someone to be there. It was just after my brother died."

"I'm sorry about that," Kate said.

"Yeah. Me, too. Did you know him?"

Boone moved closer to the kitchen entrance, making sure he was quiet.

"Yeah, I knew him. He was a hell of a soldier. And a good friend."

He didn't hear anything else, except for Milo. When Boone walked into the room, he saw the dog sitting right next to Christie's chair, scratching at his neck, which made his collar jingle.

"You guys done?" Christie asked.

"Not even close. I'm just getting Seth some coffee."

Christie nodded, then turned back to Kate. "Anyway, we met at this bar I go to sometimes. They play trivia there, and it was a nice way to spend an evening when I had nothing better to do."

"How soon did you meet him? I mean, after Nate's death."

Christie sighed behind him. "A month, I guess. I

remember it was the first night I'd been out in a long time. He gave me an answer to one of the trivia questions, then bought me a drink."

"How long did you go out?"

"A few months."

"What went wrong?"

"I don't know. Me, I guess. He wanted to help, but I didn't want all those questions. It was like going to therapy instead of a date."

"What kind of questions?"

Boone didn't even make a pretense about listening now. He got himself a coffee refill, then filled a cup for Seth, but he went to the table and sat down. He wanted to hear this.

Christie looked at him, and he could tell she was disconcerted by his presence, but he didn't care.

She cleared her throat, then looked at Kate. "About my family. My relationship with my mother and father. That kind of crap."

"Did he ask a lot of questions about Nate?"

"What do you mean by a lot?"

"Did he focus on Nate?"

"No. Just me. He thought I couldn't get close to a man because of my relationship with my mother."

"What was wrong with it?"

"Is that necessary for your profile?"

Kate sat back. "No. Sorry."

"That's okay." She bent down and petted Milo. "What are you scratching, buddy? It's really starting to get old."

Boone figured he'd better get the coffee to Seth. And that he'd best leave Kate to do her thing. "You guys take your time," he said. "Don't miss a trick. It could matter a lot."

Christie smiled at him as he stood. She nodded once, then sat up straighter. As he walked out of the room, he heard Christie talk about a guy named Brent, and Milo, scratching again.

He took his time walking down the hall. He wasn't thinking about the bugs in her room, but the man who'd been in her bed. He'd ask Kate for his last name later. It wouldn't surprise him if this Dan clown turned out to be the stalker. Psychologist. What a pussy. He'd like to see Danny boy in the field. He wouldn't last ten minutes. Jerk.

"Hey, what the hell took so long?"

Boone walked into the guest bedroom to find Seth on top of the bed, running a scan over the light fixture. "Sorry."

"They on to anything?"

"Don't know. Kate's being thorough."

"Didn't expect anything less."

"How we doing in here?"

"Give me twenty."

Boone nodded, went to the duffel and pulled out his kit, then crouched in the corner and cleaned his weapon. Seth moved around the room like smoke, getting into corners and crevices, under and over, in places Boone never would have thought to look.

Boone's electronic expertise wasn't about bugs. It was radios, GPS systems, telecommunications. When they were in the field, Boone got them where they needed to go, and got them out again. When necessary, he was the man that got the updated orders, and he was the one to report home.

Seth, on the other hand, was surveillance. He could listen to anyone, anywhere, anytime, with no one the wiser. They worked well together. They had for years.

Once Seth gave him the all clear, he knew it was safe to talk again. And there was something he really needed to know. "What do you hear from the rest?"

Seth looked at him for a long time before he went and picked up his cup of coffee. He drank, put the cup down, and walked over to Boone. Once he was crouched in front of him, he put his hand on Boone's leg. "Everyone's alive."

"Alive? Sometimes that isn't enough."

"Cade's working in Colorado. Leading tour groups through the mountains."

Boone smiled. That made sense. "What about Harper?"

"She's working in a clinic right here in L.A. Downtown. She's happy."

"Good. That's great."

"We're keeping under the radar, buddy. But this. This might turn into something ugly. And then what?"

Boone looked him right in the eye. "We prevail."

IT WAS LATE AFTERNOON BY THE time Seth was finished with every room but the kitchen. Kate and Christie were still in there, but they weren't working. They were cooking. And from what Boone could see, having a decent time of it.

He was sitting at the table, looking over some of the bugs Seth had discovered. The technology was so cutting edge it felt more like James Bond equipment than real things used by real people. But there were lots of folks out there whose sole purpose in life was to try and crawl into places they didn't belong. He should know.

Seth sat down across from him. He looked tired, but healthy. Which was good. They all needed to stay in shape.

"What's cooking?" he asked.

"Chicken and rice, with assorted vegetables," Christie said. "And for dessert? Nothing. Not even a damn piece of pie."

"Why not?" Seth asked.

"Blame your friend."

Seth slugged Boone in the arm. "You still don't get it about women and chocolate, do you, buddy?"

"Shut up. She's in training."

"Yeah, right."

Boone laughed, and Seth did, too, and it was good to hear that. He watched as Seth got out his gadgets, knowing the full sweep in the kitchen wasn't going to be made easier by the crowd, but that was okay, too. It was good to be a team, however makeshift.

"Whoa, what's this?"

Boone looked at what Seth was worried about. His scanner was pinging, but Boone couldn't tell where it was pointed. He had to look under the table. At Milo.

"Oh, shit," he said.

Seth looked at him with a shake of his head, then leaned down and petted Milo on the neck. He paused, nodded once.

"RFID?"

"Yep."

"How long has this bastard been tracking her?" Boone asked, although there was no way in hell he was ever going to have the answer.

9

"WHAT IS THAT?" Christie moved closer to Boone and Seth, who were crouched over Milo. "What are you talking about?"

Boone looked up at her. "Does Milo have an electronic dog tag?"

"No," she said. "I thought about getting one, but I wasn't sure about the side effects."

"That's what I thought," he said. He petted Milo, who rewarded him with a whimper and a lick. "Good boy." Boone stood, but Seth stayed down, manipulating Milo's neck.

"Is he hurt?" she asked, willing herself not to get crazy. It was hard, though, because it was Milo.

"No, he probably didn't feel any pain. The RFID is implanted with a needle. Only, this one feels larger. It's got broadcasting capabilities. Its own power source."

"So is he listening to us?" she asked, her voice in an involuntary whisper.

"No," Seth said. "It's not a listening device. It's a location tracker."

"He knows where we run," Boone said. "Train. Shoot."

Christie sat at the table, thinking seriously about

having a drink, even though she wasn't that fond of liquor. This was all so bizarre. The bastard was tracking them through her dog? What kind of mentally defective creep was he?

"We have to get it out of him," Seth said as he stood. "I'll get my bag."

"Wait just a minute here." Christie looked from Seth to Boone. "Are you thinking of cutting him up?"

Boone came around to her side of the table and sat next to her. "We'll make sure he isn't hurt." He looked at Seth. "You have any Novocain in there?"

"Close enough."

Christie backed away from Boone. "Are either of you veterinarians? No? Then there is no way in hell you're going near my dog with a knife. Is that clear?"

Boone looked at Seth. Kate looked at her hands. Seth scratched his head. Then he paused, and connected again with Boone. "I can fix it. But you'll have to take him to a vet to get it removed."

"What do you mean, fix it?" Christie asked.

"No knives. Nothing like that. I can disable it."

"It won't hurt Milo?"

"Milo won't feel a thing." Seth bent to his duffel.

Christie turned to Boone again, wanting to make sure that this was all legit. If something happened to Milo...

"I trust him," Boone said. "I'd let him do it to me."

"Okay. But if Milo so much as whines."

"I'll stop him." He touched her hand, and the effect was immediate and more calming than she could have imagined.

Kate got up and went to check the chicken. She got

a spoon out of the drawer and tasted the sauce, smiling her approval.

Christie liked her. She was a tough cookie, and it was good to have her on the team.

"We still have to get this room finished," Boone said, in his familiar whisper. Then he looked at Christie. "You can go in your room," he said. "Get some clothes, whatever."

"Did you throw it all out?"

"Seth is going to do that for us when he leaves. I don't want to put those sheets in your garbage."

"That's smart," she said. "Good."

"You want to go there now? Give Seth some room to finish up his work?"

"Sure." She got up, and walked with Boone down the hallway. Glancing at Seth as she walked by, she saw he had some sort of electronic device he was working on, but she had no idea what it was. If Boone trusted him, so would she. Hell, what choice did she have.

Boone moved right next to her in the hallway. He put his hand on the small of her back. A simple move meant to reassure her. It did that, but holy crap, so much more.

Everything about last night came back in a head rush. The way he looked, standing naked by the tub. The feel of his chest on her back. The way her hand had been filled with his thick cock.

"What's wrong?" he asked.

"Nothing."

"It's okay," he said softly. "I've got you."

She smiled. She'd never get tired of hearing him say that. It didn't just make her feel safe. It made her swoon.

Her grin got bigger as she thought about that. Her? Swooning? Nate would be on the floor laughing if she'd suggested such a thing. But then, he'd never have imagined her in a situation this bizarre. This terrifying.

She stopped smiling at the door. Everything inside her revolted at the idea of walking in there. Her favorite room. Her sanctuary. Defiled in a way that turned her stomach.

"Christie."

She looked at Boone. His green eyes were steady, his whole body strong and determined. But he wouldn't push her. He'd let her make the call. "Let's lock and load," she said.

In return, he graced her with that half smile of his. That, and standing by her side as she opened the door.

Of course, her gaze went straight to the bed. He'd remade it, which surprised her. Nothing fancy, just some of her sheets with a comforter she'd gotten as a gift from a client. Clean pillowcases. No trace of the red, sticky mess. No scent at all. But it wasn't her bedroom. Not anymore.

She walked past the bed, Boone at her side, and headed straight for the closet. Boone stood by the door, his shoulders looking so broad in his dark shirt. He'd pushed the sleeves up past the elbows, which made him look incredibly sexy.

Since she wanted out of there, she got right down to business. She got her suitcase from the top shelf. In it, she packed underwear and bras, and built out from there. Mostly jeans, T-shirts, and one dress that didn't need much in the way of an iron. Shoes, a pair of pajamas she doubted she'd wear. It was like packing for a trip of unknown duration. A no-frills vacation to her living room.

She turned to pull a pair of sweats down, and caught sight of Boone. He was staring at her suitcase as if mesmerized. When she looked to see what had caught his attention, it made her giggle. How do you take down an ex-Delta Force? Dazzle him with a pink thong.

She picked it up with her index finger, watching Boone as she lifted the Victoria's Secret weapon. He was spellbound. He didn't even blink.

When she dropped it back into the suitcase, his whole head moved down to catch the flutter.

Feeling wicked, she decided to test her theory further. While he was still in the trance, she undid the top button of her jeans. No effect. Then she unzipped, figuring the sound would distract him. Nope.

This would be the real test. Another thong. Would he go back and forth between thongs? Would his head just explode? She lowered her jeans, slipping them down past her hips.

Aha. He'd looked. His eyes widened quite a bit more than expected. But still, no other body movements. Well, she couldn't swear that was true. She didn't have a very good view of his fly.

She lowered her pants down past her knees and let them drop. She had to toe off her sneakers before she could take them off completely, but he didn't seem to mind. Once the jeans were off, she went to phase two. She turned around.

Normally, she wouldn't want any part of her butt exposed to this kind of light, but for this, she made an exception. When she turned her head to look back at him, bingo. She expected his eyes to *boing* out like in a cartoon.

No longer able to hold it in, she laughed. Really laughed. Jeez. How was it possible?

That, naturally, got his attention. He looked her in the eyes and blushed a deep, satisfying red.

"Busted."

He coughed, his gaze on the carpet.

"Certainly an experienced soldier like you has seen one of these babies before."

"Christie," he said, in a warning growl.

"Oh, no, big guy. I could have had my gun out and popped you right in the kneecap, and you wouldn't have noticed."

"Are you finished?"

She laughed again. "Yeah. I figured I'd eat like this." His blush renewed. "Put on some pants."

"What?"

"Please."

"My, my. Panties, huh? I'd never have guessed."

In response to her taunt, he did the mature thing. He turned his back and folded his arms across his chest.

She pulled on another pair of jeans, giggling the whole time. Was he not the cutest person ever? Of course, this wasn't over. She would have to think about this new piece of data very carefully. Strike when he least expected it.

"All clear, Rambo."

He didn't turn. But he did put his right arm out, to show her his special finger.

She closed her suitcase, then took another look

around. If she needed anything else, she wouldn't be far away, but given a choice, she wouldn't come back here. Maybe after the bastard was caught. Maybe.

"Ready?" Boone had the door open.

"As I'll ever be."

MILO SAT RIGHT NEXT TO CHRISTIE as they ate dinner, and Boone noticed she would slip him pieces of chicken as she ate. Even though it wasn't that good for the dog, Boone understood the motive. She was worried about her old pal. So was he.

Seth had explained that he was going to use a modified electromagnetic pulse to zap the RFID. It wouldn't hurt the dog, not for the duration that would be necessary. She and Boone would go to a vet first thing in the morning and get the damn thing taken out. Seth wanted it. He was going to see if he could identify the source. Figure out where the geek would have gotten it.

The other matter at hand was to lock up the doggy door, and make sure Milo never went out unattended. He'd have felt better if Seth could have taken Milo, but he didn't want to do that to Christie. She'd already been scared out of her bedroom, she didn't need to lose her best friend.

He tried to concentrate on the meal. It was good. Not enough vegetables, but still, it tasted great. He knew that was Kate's contribution. She was a hell of a cook, didn't matter what she had to work with. In Kosovo, she'd made them some incredible *cevapcici* and her *sarma* couldn't be beat.

It was great to see her and Seth working together.

After the Balkans, they'd all split up. He'd lost touch with some of them. Kate had gone deep underground. It was only a few months ago that Seth had heard from her. That first night, when she'd come back, was when she'd heard about Nate. She hadn't disappeared again. Not from them, at least.

"You know what?" Christie said. "I think I have some cookie dough in that fridge of mine."

Kate smiled. "What kind?"

"Who cares? It's cookies."

"I stand corrected."

Christie lifted her hand for a mighty high five by Kate. All Boone could do was let it go. One night of cookies wasn't going to blow her training. If he could have given her champagne to go with it, he would have. Tomorrow, they'd get back to it. Different track. Different gym, which was going to be a real pain. Different shooting range. They had to get the geek to come here. Not out there. Here, Boone had control. Here, he could take the man down, and there wouldn't be a hair follicle left for anyone to find. They just had to get him angry enough to attack.

He listened to Christie's voice as she talked so easily to Seth and Kate. He wasn't concentrating on the words, just the voice.

He'd been strong last night. He'd thought of her, focused on his responsibility. With every word she said, with every gesture of her long, graceful fingers, he felt himself weaken.

He thought again about what had happened in the closet. She'd made him stupid. It was still hard for him to reconcile that he'd held it together when she was naked and willing in his arms, but that he'd become thirteen again when he'd seen her damn panties.

Tonight would be a struggle. One he wasn't at all sure he wanted to win.

"GOOD BOY. WHAT A FINE DOG. You're the bravest of all the animals in the kingdom."

Boone smiled at Christie's chatter. She held her beloved Milo's head in her lap while Seth worked his voodoo. It took a tenth of a second and it was done. The EMP had destroyed the chip inside the RFID. The end, except for removing the chip itself.

It was also the end of the night for Seth and Kate. They'd disappear, go back to the worlds they'd created for themselves, but he knew if he needed them, they'd come back. No matter what. No matter where. They were a team.

Christie hugged them both. She invited them back under happier circumstances. No one asked what she meant. Then they were alone.

Finally and truly alone. Every bug and camera the geek had planted was gone. He'd lost his eyes and his ears. And now he'd lost his tracking system. There wasn't much left for him to do. Come back and plant more bugs? Maybe, but Boone doubted it. He'd come to claim what was his. Christie.

"I'll wash, you dry?"

She led him into the kitchen where the table was cleared and all the dishes were piled in the sink. It seemed the most natural thing in the world to grab the dishtowel, to stand, leaning against the counter, as Christie soaped up her sponge.

"So you guys were all in the Balkans, right?"

"That's right."

"With Nate."

"Yep."

She paused, her lips slightly pursed. "What did Kate do?"

"She was part of the UN peacekeeping force."

"How'd she get mixed up with you guys?"

"We had mutual acquaintances," Boone said, turning away from her.

"You mean she was a spy."

He shouldn't tell her anything. Especially when he wasn't one hundred percent certain no one was listening. "No, she wasn't. She helped the people in Kosovo."

Christie washed dishes for a while in silence, while he watched her, wanting so much to tell her everything. When she spoke, it wasn't about Kate.

"Seth, I assume, was the electronics expert, yes?"

"Surveillance."

"And you did communications, which is different."

"That's right."

"What was it you were sent over to do?"

He got another dish to dry.

"Boone?"

"I can't tell you."

"You're not even in the army anymore."

"Doesn't matter. I took an oath."

"Ah. I see. An oath."

"It matters."

"I'm sure Nate would say the same thing."

"You know how he felt about the Force."

"Yeah. He died for it."

"I can't, Christie. I'm sorry. It's not an option."

"Fine." She went on washing. Not looking at him. Bruising the china.

He put down his cloth and took her by the shoulders. He turned her to face him and made sure she was looking him straight in the eyes. "I'm not telling you because it could be dangerous for you to know. Okay? You have enough to worry about in your life without me adding to it."

She didn't respond. Her lips, which had been pressed together when she turned, loosened. Her eyes softened and he felt her relax beneath his hands. "Okay. I'm sorry I pressed. I just keep wondering why anyone would want to kill my brother. You can understand that, can't you?"

"What I can tell you is that your brother was the best of the best. What he did, he did for his country. He honored you. He honored us all. I was, I still am, proud to have served with him."

Her eyes closed. She breathed in and out slowly. When she looked at him again, it was the vulnerable Christie he'd seen so often in the last twenty-four hours, but this time, there was no fear, just sadness. "Thank you," she whispered.

Boone nodded.

She turned back, and they finished the dishes in silence. He put the towel away. Milo scratched at his locked doggy door, and Christie got quiet.

Boone took his weapon out from his jeans. "You have a leash?"

"Yeah."

"Great. I'll take him outside."

"No. Please. Not here. I'd rather take him to a park. Somewhere not around here."

"Sure, we can do that. Go get the leash. We'll be back in no time."

THEY WENT TO WESTWOOD, and walked by the university. Milo seemed no worse the wear for his implant ordeal, but Christie was silent and jumpy. It wasn't a long trip, but the ride home felt as if it took forever. He went into the house first; they both had their weapons ready and he had the scanner. They went through each room, each closet. Then they checked the locks on every door and window. Christie was so keyed up, he suggested they go to the kitchen and have some tea.

She surprised him with hot chocolate, instead. "What the hell," she said. "We already had evil cookies."

He sat her down, and they drank the sweet drink. Even he had to admit, it was damned tasty. Still, they didn't talk.

Tonight, he'd have to be vigilant. It could happen, although he doubted it would. The geek would be angry, yes. But not yet to the point of breaking. That would take a little more time. A few more trips parading for the last remaining camera—the one that focused on the path out front.

That would do it. It had to.

Christie finished her drink just as he finished his, took

their mugs to the sink and rinsed them out. Then she put the dishes away from dinner, wiped her hands and went to the door where he was waiting for her. "I'm going to take a shower," she said, turning out the kitchen light. She touched his arm. "You're welcome to join me."

Boone looked at her, into those dark brown eyes. He should say no. Offer to stand outside the bathroom until she was done. Instead, he kissed her.

10

CHRISTIE CLOSED HER EYES and sank into his kiss. Her pulse sped, but the rest of her relaxed. She felt small, protected. Amazingly turned on.

She'd thought about how he would kiss when it was just for them, not for the camera. She'd been shamefully off the mark. He teased her mouth open farther so he could slip his tongue between her teeth. He brushed her tongue with his, making her shiver, tasting of sweet chocolate. His exploration of her was intense and focused, as if this kiss would tell him all he needed to know.

What, she wondered, did he want to know about her? He knew that she was scared to death. That she'd lost her bearings and felt as if there were constant earthquakes tearing up the very ground beneath her feet. He knew she was willing, that she wanted him, that more than that, she needed him, even though the need itself confused her and made her ashamed.

His hand moved from her shoulder to the small of her back. He pulled her closer so her body and his were tight together. His erection, hard and thick, pressed against her stomach, and she remembered the feel of it in her hand.

She wanted more. To feel him between her lips, on her tongue. Inside her, pushing and urgent.

He pulled back.

She took a deep breath, then found his hand, pulling him along as she headed for the bathroom. Closing the door behind him, she closed out everything else, too. No stalker, no microchips, no warriors. Just the two of them.

"I should wait outside," he said.

"Not gonna happen."

He smiled. Not that half smile, either, but a wide, devilish grin. "And what is gonna happen?"

"I'm gonna take off all my clothes," she said.

"Oh?"

"And so are you."

"We did that last night."

"That was for comfort."

"And this?"

"Don't think so much." She backed up until she was closer to the shower. Then she pulled her T-shirt off. She'd worn one of her Wonderbras which made her look bigger than she was. It was pink and lacy, and he certainly seemed to like what he saw.

He stared as he pulled his own shirt over his head and tossed it behind him.

It was her turn to be mesmerized. She had to give it to the U.S. Army. They knew how to make their men hot as hell. Yeah, she'd seen him last night, but not for long enough, and not just standing there, letting her stare with abandon.

She toed off her sneakers and her socks, which wasn't

terribly easy, at least not while trying to look sexy. But then, he had to crouch down to get his shoes off.

While he was down there, she figured she'd make it worth his while. She undid her jeans, and pushed them down and off.

He looked up. Got really still. She, wearing her mind-snapping thong, moved in close. Boone just looked for a long moment, his lips slightly parted, then his hands came up to the side of her panties and he pulled them down. He wasn't in a hurry.

She heard him moan as the panties dropped to the floor. At first she thought he was going to ignore her and glom on to the thong, but he wasn't much interested in anything but her.

His hands moved up her outer thighs as he looked up at her face. "You're a dangerous woman," he said.

"Me?"

He nodded.

"I can't even hit the target."

"Don't kid yourself." He rose, his hands still on her hips. "You've got one hell of an arsenal."

"I'd feel a lot better if I could shoot straight."

"You'll learn. I'll teach you."

"That's actually not what I want to learn right now."

He kissed her again. Slow, deep. Thorough.

She used the opportunity to undo his jeans and push them down as far as she could without stopping the kiss. Boone took over. She felt him kick away his pants to join his shirt.

It was her turn to break away. She opened the shower door and turned on the water. As she did that he undid the hooks of her bra. It ended up on the pile, and they were both, finally, naked.

"God, you're beautiful," he whispered, nuzzling behind her ear.

"You think so?"

"I do."

She turned into his chest, at once liking that he was so tall, and wishing she didn't have to look up so high to see his face. "You're not bad yourself."

With his hands on her shoulders he held her steady, looked at her with serious eyes. "I shouldn't do this."

"You think he can get in here? Into this room without you knowing about it?"

"No. But you can make me lose my concentration."

"I can? Wow, I had no idea."

"Just thinking about you in that little thong of yours…"

"I meant to ask you about that. Panty fetish?"

"Nope. Not that I've noticed. Before today, that is."

"Ah, so it's *my* panties that had you so rapt."

He nodded. "Guess so."

"I don't understand why you're not taken. I really don't. You're gorgeous, you're smart. You've got that whole dark and dangerous thing going."

"I told you. I can't. Things are complicated."

"You know what's not complicated?"

"What?"

She kissed him again, only this time, she moved her hand down, fisting his hot erection. "Let's get clean so we can get dirty," she said, her mouth a scant inch from his. "Show me what you like. Teach me how to please you."

"You already are," he said, reaching behind her so he

could open the shower door wide enough for both of them to get in.

The water was perfect and it hit them from three sides. Of course, the nozzles were adjusted to her height, but Boone didn't seem to mind. He touched her back with both hands, rubbed her chest with his, the water and the heat making everything slick.

She reached for the soap, but he stopped her with his teeth on her neck. It was a very effective move, stilling her instantly. He growled as he held her there, his left hand moving down her stomach, between her legs.

He didn't need the shower or the soap to make her wet and slick down there. His finger was large, blunt but practiced, as he explored her. First finding her clit, then sliding back until he pushed in, filling her so well she rose on her toes.

Now he held her with that finger, which was powerful motivation not to move. When he looked at her, she could barely see the green of his eyes, they were so dark with his excitement.

She wanted more than his finger. To let him know, she squeezed him, enough to make his eyebrows raise in surprise.

She gave him her most wicked look. "Oh, yeah."

"Well, you're going to have to wait."

"Why?"

"Because I said so."

She coughed at his audacity. "And if I don't want to?"

"I'll enjoy the show."

She snuck her hand between them and tweaked the hell out of his nipple.

"Hey, that hurt."

"And there's more where that came from, so watch your step, buddy."

"You think you can take me?"

"I can try."

The grin came slowly, as did the delight in his eyes. "You're right. Let's get clean and get the hell out of here. I want you on your back."

"Nope."

"Why not?"

She tweaked his other nipple. "'Cause I like to be on top."

Boone grabbed her wrist. There was no possibility of her getting loose if he didn't want her that way. Not that she minded. She might be hell on wheels when it came to business, but in the bedroom? She liked to be dominated. In the right way, of course. So far, Boone had the perfect balance.

She thought about the difference, last night to now. A lot had happened, and she'd been on an emotional roller coaster. He hadn't missed a beat. Last night, he'd called it so right it was spooky. Tonight… Oh, yeah.

"What was that again?" he asked.

"I said, I like to be on top. If you can't handle that, well, then I guess I won't get clean at all."

He spun her around and brought her back up against his body. She could feel how the game excited him. How he liked feeling his own strength. "If you won't wash yourself, I guess I'll have to."

He reached behind her to the basket where she kept her sponges and bath soaps. He took the biggest of the sponges in his free hand and, still holding her, she knew he faced a dilemma. His solution was pretty ingenious, actually. He pulled his body away from hers far enough to put the sponge in the space. Then he got the soap, opened the top with his teeth, and squeezed enough for three baths onto the sponge.

She laughed, which made him grin, but he didn't give an inch. She wasn't going anywhere, which was a good thing. Because as soon as he put back the soap, he got the sponge and started washing her.

Being a man, he chose the good parts first.

She used the sponge all the time, but it never felt like it did as he washed her breasts in slow circles, first one and then the other, avoiding the brush across her nipples she craved. When she tried to maneuver herself into the right path, he stopped the sponge altogether, until she relaxed and let him have his way. "Tease," she whispered.

He leaned in close to her ear. "Count on it." He moved the sponge down, the soap dripping over her stomach, down her thighs. Using his foot, he pushed her legs apart.

Even though she knew it was useless to fight it, she did. She had to. But he got her feet planted more than shoulder-width apart, and with her wrist still captive, held her steady.

In order to reach his next objective, he had to bend over her, his chest slippery with soap, his cock pressed up and slightly into the cleft of her ass. It was incredibly difficult not to squirm, to just let him have this power.

To make things worse, or maybe better, he gripped her earlobe between his teeth, just hard enough. His breath, ragged now, sounded practically feral.

She closed her eyes, feeling everything. The size of his hands, the way his broad shoulders dwarfed her own, the slippery cock so close and yet not nearly close enough.

He brought the sponge between her legs, rubbing back and forth, keeping it light, making her insane.

She struggled to break his hold, but he wouldn't let up, not an inch. The struggle itself brought her a little relief; it made him rub harder with the sponge. Just not hard enough. "Boone, please."

"Please what?"

"Let me go."

"Is that what you want?"

"Yes."

He did as she asked. One second she was enveloped in his strength, then next she was adrift. Turning slowly, the water hitting her sensitive skin, but not bringing her any pleasure, she looked up into his eyes.

"Take me to bed," she said. "Any way you want me."

He took hold of her again, by her shoulders, and crushed her mouth in a bone-melting kiss. Her surrender was complete, and she'd never felt more taken care of in her life.

Boone came up for air, but it took him longer to come back to his senses. All he wanted was to lift her up against the wall and make love to her until they both melted down the drain. But that wasn't gonna happen. Not like that. His first priority was her safety. He was just having a hard time convincing his dick.

"Come on. Let's go," he said, turning off the water. "You get dry. I'm going to go out, check the house. I'll bring you back something clean to wear."

Christie blinked at him as if he were speaking a foreign language. "What?"

He stepped out of the shower and grabbed the first big bath sheet off the rack. Then back in, where he wrapped her up. "Christie?"

"You're leaving without me?"

"Just for a minute. I have to check the house. With all the precautions we took, I'm sure everything's fine. But I'm not taking any chances, okay?"

"Can't I go with you?"

"Not yet. Soon." He stepped to the carpet again, getting a towel for himself and doing a crappy job of drying off. It was hell pulling up his jeans. He hadn't lost his erection, and that's the way he wanted it, but damn, the zipper. He left the top button undone, grabbed his gun, took the safety off, and headed for the door. Just as he reached for the knob, he changed his mind, went back and kissed Christie one more time, deep hard and fast. Then he got out of there before he lost his mind.

The second he was in the hallway, he was all business. If the geek had gotten in the house, Boone would know it quickly, just by checking one panel in his bag. There was no entry and no exit from this house that wouldn't trip a silent alarm, and give him ample opportunity to deal with the situation. At least that was the plan.

Gun up, Spidey sense on full alert, he went down the hallway so silently Milo didn't even look up. "Good dog," Boone whispered as he got next to the animal, who had his big paw over Boone's bag.

Milo didn't seem to mind being moved. Boone

flipped back the bag flap and there was the panel, all green, all clear. He relaxed, but not by much. While he trusted Seth with his life, he wasn't quite that sure about electronics. So he went room to room, into closets, checking under furniture, behind cabinets.

It took a while, and he hoped Christie wasn't too cold or impatient. He hadn't lost his hard-on, which made him wonder if he was a little too fond of his job. He knew he was too fond of her.

Coward that he was, he chose not to think about that tonight. Maybe tomorrow he'd face the fact that he should never have kissed her. But tonight? He was going to get that woman on her back. For starters.

The house was clear. Nothing had been disturbed, no one was even interested. Seth had set up a camera in the backyard, on both sides of the house, and across the street. Good man, that Seth.

Boone put the safety back on as he headed to the bathroom. He tapped the door so he wouldn't startle her, then he walked in.

Christie was sitting on the edge of the tub, still wrapped in the towel. She'd combed her hair away from her face. When she looked up at him, he stopped dead still. Her eyes were wide with a trust that made him want to slay dragons. Her lips, sweet and ripe, were parted, showing a hint of her even, white teeth. She stood, pale shoulders trembling. And as he stared at her with his heart in fifth, she dropped the towel.

"Oh, shit," he said, surprised that he could form the words.

"Come on, soldier boy. Show me what you got."

He was at her side before she could blink. He picked her up, careful not to hurt her in his panic. They were out the door and down the hallway, and he was raging for her, hoping like hell Milo cleared the room before he got hurt.

Then they were at the edge of the mattress, and he went to his knees. But he couldn't let her go. While she was still cradled in his arms, he kissed her again. His tongue thrust into her hard, a preview of what was to come.

He felt nails on his back, swallowed her moan. There was no choice, he had to let her go so he could rip his goddamn jeans off.

Christie had the same idea. The moment she was on the bed, her fingers were at his zipper. He had to stop her though because this wasn't going to be easy. He was so hard, he'd have to watch it or become a soprano.

He didn't even mind her laughter as he carefully unzipped. Once he was free, he was out of those Levi's in two hot seconds. That's what he wanted. To be next to her, on her, in her.

She welcomed him with another moan, spreading her legs so he could climb between them. Every touch was torture as his cock wanted only one thing.

When her hand circled him, he groaned, it was that intense. "Come on, Boone. Come home."

He felt the soft wetness between her legs and he thrust so hard she screamed. He covered her mouth with his, swallowing her breath, her passion, and he reached down and lifted her legs. Right there, that was it. He used his knees to balance and every muscle in his body to take it home, hard.

Her hands were on his back, her nails sharp and exactly right. He liked the pain, loved knowing he could do this to her, stretch her like this, make her cry out over and over. There was nothing but her slick heat, nothing but the taste of her cries. He knew he was hurting her shoulders, pressing too hard, but he couldn't stop. It wasn't just his cock, it was every part of him, his legs, his chest, his mind, and he was in her, in her, harder, deeper.

She bit his lip, she tore at his flesh and her heels beat on his back. All of it was perfect.

There was no more time, no control at all. "I can't," he growled, knowing he wasn't making sense.

"Do it," she said. Then she grabbed his head between her hands and she kissed him, assaulting his mouth, tearing at his lips.

He shouted as he came, as hard as he had ever in his life.

She never let up, milking him beyond the point of pain all the way to insanity.

He reared back, gritting his teeth, his whole chest pounding with his heart. His cock pulsing at the same beat.

She pushed him. Her hands weren't on his back anymore, but on his chest. And she was pushing him, struggling, and he must be hurting her, but he didn't know how.

He pulled out, checked where his elbows were, his knees. He couldn't be pulling her hair, so what the hell?

"Move, goddammit!" she yelled, shoving him harder than he would have thought possible.

He sat up on his knees, and she was staring at his

chest, kicking at him, pushing him, and then he looked down and he saw it. The red dot. Right over his heart.

He rolled just as the shot shattered the window.

11

"GET DRESSED."

Christie stared at the hole in her wall. One second later, and Boone would have been dead. One second.

She felt a warm drip down the inside of her thigh, and she realized that they hadn't discussed birth control. That she hadn't even thought about him wearing a rubber. She took the pill, had for years, but she always insisted that the guy be safe. Always. But not with Boone, and Boone had almost been killed. If she hadn't looked down. If she hadn't seen all those TV shows with the laser sights, she wouldn't have known. She wouldn't have warned him.

"Christie."

She looked up. Boone, sweat making his face shiny, stared at her. He had his gun out.

"Christie, I'm okay. You need to get dressed. Right now."

She moved on the bed, sore from the most incredible orgasm she could ever remember. "I'll go turn on the shower."

"No. There's no time. Just get your clothes on. Just hurry."

She nodded. Turned on her elbow to get up. But his hand on her shoulder stopped her.

"Stay low. I don't know where he's shooting from, I don't know what he can see. So stay low, grab your clothes and get to the hallway."

She moved in slow motion, finding her shirt, jeans, bra, panties, shoes. Then she crawled on her own carpet to the hallway, expecting a bullet in her back the whole way.

She bumped into Milo and nearly screamed, but he just licked her face, huddling close, his tail wagging. She hugged him tight, then struggled into her clothes, watching as Boone made his way to the window.

How could the bastard have seen them? The blinds were drawn, so how could he see? Was his timing on purpose? Was he watching them make love, just waiting until they came to shoot Boone? If she hadn't seen the red dot, then Boone would have fallen on her body. He would have still been inside her.

She was shaking, so damn hard she couldn't hook her bra. There was no way she was going to cry. Not while he could see her. Not while that asshole was outside, looking in.

"Where's your purse?"

"What?"

Boone didn't look at her. He was almost to the window, and she could make out the muscles in his back, in his thighs. He didn't touch the blinds, but she saw where the bullet had broken through. She could see the glint of glass on the carpet.

Even the blood on the bed hadn't felt like this. Hadn't ripped the last shred of safety from the edges of her mind. Finally, she got the bra on and then she put her shirt over her head. The moment of blackness nearly made her pass out, but she didn't cry.

"Your purse. Where's your purse?"

"In the kitchen."

"Are you dressed?"

"I don't have my shoes on."

"That's okay. Can you get to your purse without standing up? Can you keep clear of the windows?"

"I think— Yeah. I can."

"Do that. Carefully. Then get your keys out, okay?"

"Okay."

He looked at her. "Keep it together, Christie. I've got you."

She nodded, thought about putting on her sneakers, but she headed for the kitchen on hands and knees. Milo trotted along with her, trying to get her attention, but she ignored him. Inch by inch she crawled until she saw her purse next to her chair. She'd put it there so casually, not ever thinking that it was out of the line of sight of a sniper.

There was no sound at all from the other room. All she wanted to do was turn, see Boone, just for a second. Make sure he was still there. Still alive. But she kept moving until she could touch the edge of her purse, feel the leather strap in her hand.

If her heart would just stop pounding, she'd catch her breath and it would be okay. It wouldn't hurt so much. She brought her purse up to her chest, and crawled back to the hallway, instantly better when she saw that Boone was fine.

He wasn't naked anymore. He had on jeans and he was pulling on a pair of socks.

Socks. She hadn't gotten socks, and she hated to wear her sneakers without socks, but she couldn't get them now. The tears she'd been fighting broke through. She swiped them away, pissed that she was crying over stupid socks.

"Christie?"

She sniffed, swiped. "Yeah."

"You have the purse?"

"Yes."

"Get out your car keys."

"Okay." She opened her purse and found her keys, but she had to hold them in her fist because they made so much noise.

"Now make sure Milo follows, and head for the garage door, okay? Keep low. Take your purse, and go to the door, but don't open it, you understand?"

"Yeah. Okay. You're coming, right?"

"I'll be right there."

She didn't have to encourage Milo. He'd caught on that things weren't good, and he was sticking close to the pack, his tail between his legs, his nose low to the ground. She knew just how he felt.

When they got to the door that led into the garage, Christie realized she hadn't taken her shoes, which made weeping over socks seem pretty ridiculous.

She put her back against the wall, her purse on her chest, her arms over her purse. Her bare feet were flat on the cold floor. Milo sat in front of her, his head on his paws, his eyes staring up at her.

There was no noise, no sound at all. Boone would come in a second. Any second. She started counting, keeping the rhythm steady. *Ten, eleven, twelve...*

When she got to eighty, she realized she'd left her gun in the living room. So when the bastard broke in, she'd be here, barefoot and helpless. All that training for nothing. What did it matter? She couldn't hit the target. She'd have missed him anyway.

"You okay?"

She jumped against the door, then realized it was Boone, and he was still with her. "Can we go now?"

"We can. Let's just do this by the book, okay?" He was coming toward her, crouched but not crawling, wearing his shirt, a leather jacket, holding his duffel under his left arm, his gun in his right hand. "You need to carry my bag and give me the keys."

She nodded.

"Christie, honey? The keys?"

She passed them over, and took his duffel, which was incredibly heavy.

"Can you do it?"

"Yes."

"All right. No lights. Just let Milo in the backseat, then you get into the passenger seat. Put your seat belt on the second you close the door.

"Where are we going?"

"I'll tell you when we're clear. Right now, just concentrate on getting in the car."

She nodded, wishing she'd remembered her shoes.

Boone opened the door. She stood, feeling that target in the center of her back. She headed out, Milo on her heels, and did exactly as she was told. Boone got behind the wheel, pressed the outer garage button, then turned the key.

This, she was familiar with. The darting out, the escape. But the last time she'd had to do it she'd been alone. There'd been no hole in her wall.

They hit the street in a screech of tires, then he pressed the button, and put the car in Drive. She had to hold on, despite the seat belt, as he jetted forward. She didn't let go until they were on the San Diego Freeway.

"Are you okay?"

"No, I'm not okay," she said. "I forgot my shoes. And you were almost killed."

"But you're not hurt?"

"No. How did he know where to shoot?"

"There are ways. I'm guessing he drilled a hole in the wall, very small, sent a tiny camera through."

"Seth didn't find it?"

"No, he didn't. I don't know why. Seth is really good at what he does."

"Not good enough."

Boone put his hand on her thigh. "You saved my life."

"I suppose so."

"Thank you."

She nodded, but she couldn't speak. Not without breaking down, and dammit, she wouldn't. No more crying. The bastard had chased her out of her home.

"We're going to my place," he said. "We'll regroup. We'll figure this thing out, and we'll get him. I swear to God, we'll get him."

She stared out the window at the passing cars. She had

no idea what time it was. It didn't matter. She didn't have to be at work in the morning, so who cared how late it was? She didn't have to go to the cleaners, or meet with clients, or call her friends, or go to her book club. All she had to do was stay alive. And that wasn't looking so good.

BOONE KEPT IT TOGETHER ALL the way to Pasadena. It took a hell of a long time, because he used every maneuver he knew, checking for tails all the way across Los Angeles. He wished she would say something.

Who the hell was this guy? What did he want with her?

He turned onto Del Mar, slowing the car down to check the rearview mirror.

"Is this it?" Christie said, shocking the hell out of him. "Am I on the run now? Is this my new life?"

"No. We'll be going back to the house."

"Are you nuts?"

"It's the only way we'll catch him. We have to get him there."

"No. I'm not going back there."

"It'll be safe."

"That's what you said right before he nearly shot you."

He wanted to reassure her, but he didn't know how. "Let's get together with Seth and Kate. We'll talk it through. If you don't want to go back, of course you don't have to. No one will force you."

"You can't go back, either."

"Yeah, I can."

"He can see through the goddamn walls. And he meant to kill you, not me. You."

"To get to you."

She turned back to the window. He didn't blame her. He'd been wrong about this guy from day one, and for the life of him, he couldn't figure out how. How could a stalker get equipment like that? The only thing that made sense was that he wasn't an ex-spook. He was working for the Company. Now. And if he was with the Company, than chances were good he knew who Boone was. Not just Boone, but Kate and Seth.

"Where the hell are we?" she asked, her voice still bitter.

"Almost at my place."

"Do you have any food there?"

"Not a thing."

"Shit."

He smiled, he couldn't help it. "Tell you what. I'll have Seth bring you whatever you want."

"Great. I want cheesecake. And diet soda. And I want size-seven Nikes with cotton socks."

"Tonight, you'll have cheesecake. I'm not so sure about the shoes."

She sniffed, still not looking his way. "Fine."

He approached his driveway carefully, studying the cars on either side of the street. He recognized all but one, and that was in front of Walter's place. Slowing the car, he looked at Walter's windows. The only one that was lit was upstairs. The bedroom.

He turned into his drive and went past the main house to his little place. It had once been a garage, but it had been converted to a guest house before he'd moved in. It was quiet, and hidden from the street.

Christie got out as soon as he'd parked, and she let

Milo out, too. The dog investigated the small patch of grass by the front door.

Boone checked his tell, the thin wire he threaded between the door and the frame. It hadn't been disturbed. Once he'd unlocked the door, he went in, weapon drawn, and checked each room. It didn't take long. The place had one bedroom, his office, the kitchen, bath, living room. Nothing was out of place. No one had triggered his motion sensor. He went back to the car, got his duffel, and went to stand next to Christie. "I'll have Seth bring Milo some dog food."

She nodded. "Don't forget the cheesecake."

"I won't. We need to go in, though. I have to make some calls."

She called Milo, and the three of them went into the house. Milo investigated with his nose, and Christie with her hands. She touched things, his lamp, the top of the club chair, his books.

He knew it wasn't a nice place, but at least it was clean. It had never felt like a home. Like everything else in his life, it was a temporary measure, somewhere to hole up while he tried to find his life.

Seth had a place just like it. Quiet, hard to find. So did Kate, and the others. They were displaced persons. Exiles in their own country.

He understood Christie's despair. It felt like hell to be banished. But for Christie, it was a question of finding one man. A clever man, a player, yes, but one man. And once they got him, she'd get everything back. Boone and his friends would have to find deeper holes to hide in, but Christie would be all right.

He went to his office and looked up Walter's phone number. He had all the neighbors in his book, listed along with what they drove, if they had pets, where they worked. Walter answered after the first ring. He sounded drunk.

"Hey, Walter. It's Boone. You in the mood for a couple games of pool?"

"I got company."

"Oh, sorry. Have a good one."

Walter hung up, but Boone knew the car out front belonged to Walter's friend.

The next call was to Seth. It was short, filled with several heartfelt curses, and instructions for a grocery run. Kate was sleeping, but as soon as Boone told her what happened, she was alert, and on her way. The calls made, he went in search of Christie.

She was standing in the kitchen. "You need a decorator."

"Yeah, I do. But not for here. This is just a room. It doesn't need to be fancy."

She turned to him. "Fancy? How about livable? This is like a prison cell."

"I have cable."

"So does Leavenworth."

"Hey, at least it has a coffee machine." He got the grounds out of the freezer, then fixed a full pot. They'd be up late tonight, and they'd need the caffeine. Seth was bringing cream along with some other necessities. Boone had a lot of protein powder and PowerBars, but he didn't have anything fresh. He cleaned out the fridge before every job.

"It wouldn't take much, you know. A little paint, a

couple of inexpensive pictures for the walls. It has to be hard, waking up in this place. Boone, you deserve better."

"I'll have better. Just not here."

"Care to explain that?"

"Why don't I get you a pair of socks. Your feet must be cold." He walked out of the kitchen, with Christie right behind.

"Wait a minute. What the hell's with you? You live like a monk. You have all this spy stuff. You're not in the service anymore. What happened in the Balkans, Boone?"

He turned and put his hands on her shoulders. "I can't tell you. And it's not important now. We have a lot to do tonight, and we have to be focused on only one thing. Getting that prick, taking him down. Got it?"

She nodded, but she didn't look happy about it.

He went to the dresser and pulled out a pair of thick socks, but when he went to give them to her she was standing by his bed.

"This is just sad," she said, looking at his plain white sheets and old, plaid blankets. There was no headboard. Just a side table, where he kept his gun, and on top of the dresser, a secondhand television.

"I've slept in worse places."

She sat down to put on the socks, but she studied him. "You bring women here?"

"No."

"You don't date?"

"Not so's you'd notice."

"Come on, Boone. A healthy guy like you? I can't picture you embracing a life of celibacy."

He had no reason to, but he felt embarrassed. "I'm not."

"Who, besides me?"

"Do we have to talk about this?"

"No, we don't. We don't have to say another word."
She got up, went into the living room and sat on the floor
next to Milo.

Feeling like a total shit, he went to sit beside her. He
thought about asking her to join him on the couch, but
this would be fine. "Sorry."

"You have nothing to apologize for. You put your life
at risk for me, and you don't even know me. I'm sure
I'm keeping you from your regular work, so you're not
even making any money."

"That doesn't matter."

"Of course it matters." She turned to face him. "How
much would you charge for this if I wasn't Nate's sister?"

"Nothing."

"Liar. Don't do that to me. Someday, in theory, I'll
have my life back. I'll have a job. I want to pay you."

That bothered him more than he understood. It
wasn't an outrageous thing to offer. He was, in fact,
losing money on the deal. "Can't you just accept that
this is something I want to do?"

"Yes. Which doesn't negate my need to pay you. I'm
pretty damn helpless, in case you haven't noticed.
Paying you, even if it is in the future, will at least let me
feel like I have something to contribute. Some tiny bit
of control."

"Fair enough."

"So?"

He took a deep breath as he looked at her. She was
a beautiful woman. Strong, sensible and full of courage.

He admired her, and he'd always remember making love with her, even if the ending wasn't the warm cuddle it should have been. He wouldn't forget what a horrible mistake it was, either. He could have gotten them both killed. It wouldn't happen again.

"Hello? You still here?"

"Sorry. I got lost for a minute."

"I could see that." She touched his cheek. "Where were you?"

"I didn't have a chance to tell you before. You were amazing."

She smiled. "We were. Despite the worst ending ever."

"It could have been worse."

She shuddered, and the smile disappeared. "So what do I owe you?"

"Two thousand."

"If that's all you charge, no wonder you have no good furniture."

"The job's not over. Let's start with two and go from there."

"Fair enough." She leaned in just enough to let him know she'd welcome a kiss to seal the deal.

It couldn't happen. Not tonight. Not ever again. He got up and went to get them coffee.

12

CHRISTIE SAT WITH HER FEET pulled up on the chair and her arms around her knees as she waited for Seth and Boone to put the groceries away.

She should help, but she didn't want to. Mostly, she wanted to crawl into a hole and never come out.

"I didn't know which cheesecake to get," Seth said, "so I got a couple."

That made her look. He'd picked up plain and strawberry, which perked her up a little. So did the big box of Lucky Charms he pulled out of the bag.

Boone had remembered. A really considerate, sweet thing to do. Now that things were a little calmer, she'd thought about before the gunshot. The sex.

She tried to remember when she'd made love like that. She'd actually come with no extra help. Usually—no, always—she couldn't. She either asked her companion to give her some specialized attention, or she brought out the vibrator. It wasn't necessarily a bad thing, just the way she was built. Or so she'd thought.

Maybe it was how he was built, or how he'd lifted her legs. Or maybe it was because he was Boone.

No. She wasn't going there. Boone wasn't the magic

one, he was the temporary hero, which was different. This was a traumatic time, and she was clinging to him for dear life. It would be a terrible mistake to romanticize things. He certainly wasn't.

A knock at the door brought two weapons into play. It was totally automatic, like covering her mouth when she sneezed. Both Boone and Seth were ready to react in a heartbeat, ready to kill, if necessary. Professional soldiers without a war. Which begged the question, how could the military let these particular soldiers go?

She knew something about their training. It was the most vigorous, brutal routine there was. Delta Force was focused on terrorism, and these men knew how to handle situations from stopping a sniper to foiling an airplane hijacking. They knew how to use every kind of weapon from knives to high explosives. CIA operatives had nothing on Delta Force when it came to surveillance and tracking. If anything, the army should be begging them to come back, not making them hide.

Nate had refused to talk about it. Even when she'd used her sister card, he kept his mouth shut. She knew, though, that whatever had gone down in the Balkans had been seriously bad. Afterward, Nate, who'd always been meticulous about his appearance, had become sloppy about his clothes. He hadn't had a haircut, which was totally bizarre, because he thought the ladies loved his cut. The last time they'd talked, he'd been sullen and nervous, and he'd barely eaten, even though he was as thin as she'd ever seen him.

Kate walked in, and she nodded at Christie before she

got a cup of coffee. The three of them sat down at the table, Boone to her left. Seth and Kate had notebooks and pens.

"So what the hell happened?" Kate asked.

"Wait," Boone said. "Christie, why don't you get something to eat. Refill your coffee."

She nodded. "Anyone else want cheesecake?"

Seth did, so she served up a couple of slices before she sat down.

By that time, Kate had pulled out a spreadsheet. On it was everything she'd found out about every man Christie had dated.

But before they got to that, Seth wanted to know what had happened at the house.

"The geek knew we were in the living room. He had a scoped rifle, I'm thinking an M24. Laser scope. He had a bead right on my chest, so he wasn't aiming blind."

"He had a camera."

Boone nodded as Seth cursed. He'd eaten half his dessert, but now he pushed it away as if he didn't deserve it.

"I don't know how I could have missed it. I went through that house with a fine-tooth comb."

Boone sighed. "I'm pretty sure he drilled, sent in a pinhole on a fiber-optic cable. I don't think it was there until after you left."

Seth crossed his arms. "Then we shouldn't have left."

"The point is, we have to find this guy. Now. Not later. He's accelerating, but he's not entering. What does that tell us?"

"He's a coward," Kate said.

"True. What else?"

"His objective is to terrify and control."

Boone nodded. "He wants me, us, out of the way. So he can have her to himself."

"To do what? Own her?" Kate asked. "Or is this revenge?"

Now it was Christie's turn to push away her cheesecake. It turned her stomach, how they were talking about her, but she knew it was necessary. If they wanted to stop the bastard, they had to dissect his motivations. She just wasn't sure she was strong enough to hear them.

"You okay?"

Boone was concerned, his hand over hers, that crease above his nose deep.

"I think I'm going to go watch TV with Milo. Call if you need me." She left the room and went right to the bedroom, to Boone's sad bed. Milo trotted in, and she coaxed him up next to her. Then she looked around for the remote.

"Is this what you're looking for?"

Boone stood near the dresser, holding the remote.

"Yeah, thanks."

He walked it over to her and sat on the edge of the bed. "You should try and get some sleep."

She shrugged.

"Don't give up. These are the best people I know."

"What if he's better?"

"He isn't."

She hugged Milo. "Go on. I'll be fine."

Boone looked at her for a long time, then he stood and put his gun on the bedside table. "You can use this until we get back to your place."

She watched his back as he left the room, then she turned to the gun. It was too much to think about. Guns and what she used to think of as home. She picked up the remote and turned on the TV. She hadn't thought of TV in weeks, if not months. It was so bright and loud. The people looked happy. Normal. How could the world go on when hers had turned upside down? She lay down, hugging the pillow instead of the dog. And she smelled Boone. His scent was in the sheets. It wasn't a cologne, it was the man. Completely distinct, she'd know it anywhere.

She closed her eyes and breathed deeply, oddly comforted.

TERROR PROPELLED HER UP THE bed where her head cracked against the wall. A hand touched her shoulder, a chest pressed against her side and her breath ran out before her scream.

"Christie, it's me. Christie."

She gasped as she struggled against him, the voice familiar but it was dark and her heart pounded so hard it hurt her chest.

"Shh, Christie, honey, it's okay."

Her fingers released the blanket and grabbed on to Boone's shirt. It ripped as she forced him closer, needing to feel him, to make him real. He touched her hair, her side, and she pulled as if she could climb right inside him.

"It's okay, it's all right," he said, over and over, until the words made sense and she didn't feel as if she were going to die.

Her mouth found his and she breathed him in, and still he wasn't near enough. Her hand went to his neck, her leg wrapped around his hips and she needed him so much.

If he hadn't kissed her back, she would have cried until the ocean was dry, but he did, he kissed her, hard and deep.

What she needed was Boone, just Boone. Only him, and no one else. Her hand went under his shirt to touch his warm skin. She pressed her palm over his heart but she couldn't find the beat.

He thrust again into her mouth, his tongue rigid and thick, and she captured him between her teeth and sucked hard, making him moan and push up with his hips.

Her hand moved from his chest to his waist, to the panic of getting him unbuttoned and unzipped. He went to help and she shoved him away.

When she released his tongue, he pulled back, away from her, and it didn't matter because she had his zipper down and when she reached inside his pants he was hard and ready.

"Christie," he said, his voice a coarse growl, warning her.

"Don't," she said. "Don't you dare."

"You had a nightmare. You're scared."

She held him in her fist, almost squeezing. "Damn right I'm scared. You were almost killed. You got that? Killed. It could all be over in a heartbeat, and I'm not going down empty, you hear me? I won't."

"Stop it," he said. "You're not going to die. I'm not going to let you die."

She pumped him with one hand, the other went to his waistband to push his pants down and off. When she couldn't push any farther, she reached for her own, desperate to be naked, to have him inside her.

"Christie. Wait."

"No. Don't."

"I'm not leaving you, I swear to God. Just slow down. Take a breath."

"Go to hell," she said as she pushed her pants down her thighs.

"I'm not going anywhere, I told you," he said, his hand circling her wrist.

It was dark, so she couldn't see his face well, and she couldn't tell if he was mad, but he wanted her, she knew that, so what the hell was his problem?

"Talk to me, honey. Tell me what scared you so badly."

"What scared me? Haven't you been paying attention?" She jerked her wrist free. "I don't want to talk. I want to screw. Now."

"I don't."

She reached for his cock again, but he stopped her before she touched him. "Liar."

"I don't want to screw. Not now, not with you."

"Don't preach at me, dammit."

"I'm not. I just want you to slow down. We can do whatever you want. But let's take our time, okay?"

She pulled away from him completely, kicking off the stupid blankets and her pants. Naked from the waist down, except for his socks, she wanted to laugh at herself, but she was so afraid that it wouldn't be laughter at all.

Boone was right, she had been dreaming. This time, she hadn't seen the red dot in time. Boone had fallen over her body, dead, and his blood had been hot and thick, like the blood all over her bed.

Why couldn't she stop shaking? Boone was alive, and the blood on the bed was fake, so why did she feel as if she were going to be sick if she didn't do something right now?

He touched her shoulder, making her jump. "Okay?"

She nodded, and his hand gentled. It was so large and warm. If she just focused on his touch, she'd be okay. She'd stop trembling.

He moved over so he was sitting beside her. His legs touched hers and she didn't even care that he was still dressed. She leaned over, pressing herself against the hard bulk of his body.

His arm slipped around her shoulder. And then, with his other hand, he touched her face. He was so tender, she cried out. Tears came then, and he kept stroking her cheek, whispering soft words that meant nothing and everything. She tried to stop, but there was no stopping. The tears poured out of her, wracking sobs that shook her so that she didn't feel the old trembling at all. Boone brought her closer but never stopped touching her.

Finally, she was empty. The only thing holding her together was the arm around her shoulder, the touch of gentle, coarse fingers against her skin. She looked up into his face, and even though it was dark and there were shadows all around her, she saw the kindness in his eyes. He knew. He understood.

He came toward her slowly, still patient and watching, until his lips brushed hers. The panic was over and now she understood his caution. This was what she'd wanted all along. To be close, to be cared for.

He kissed her more deeply, letting her know that there was no rush, that she was safe. Only when she parted her lips did she feel his desire, hot and sweet on her tongue.

For a long time, they just kissed. As the seconds drifted by, everything outside faded and she felt herself relax deep inside. When her hand went to his thigh, he didn't try to stop her. She stretched her fingers out but they didn't reach all the way across. The memory of him in the bathtub, before they'd made love, when he'd given her comfort. She pulled back, wishing she'd turned on the light. "Are you sure you're a soldier?"

He laughed softly. "I'm pretty sure."

"How'd you get to be so nice?"

"I'm not that nice."

"Liar."

He shook his head, and then he kissed her again. A long, slow, deep kiss as they fell backward onto the awful bed. He lifted her shirt, patiently moving first the right side, then the left. They parted, but only so he could pull it over her head. Where it went after that, she had no idea. But the move did rouse her to finish the job she'd started before. His jeans were already undone, so she pulled and tugged until they were off.

Eventually, they were naked. Boone had maneuvered them into the traditional position, then pulled the covers up to their waists. She rested now, her head in the crook of his arm, her leg curled over his, touching as much of him as she could.

"It's late," he said.

"So?"

"You have to be exhausted."

She moved her hand down to his cock. Bless his little testosterone-laden body, he was still hard. "Make love to me until I fall asleep."

He laughed again, but a moment later, he was over her, his legs between hers, his hands on either side of her head. One kiss, fast, then a nibble on her chin. Before she could even react, he'd moved down to her chest, to her breasts, and his tongue painted slow circles around and around, coming near, but not touching her nipples.

She reached for him and tugged at his hair, letting him know that teasing was fine and good, but damn.

A quick study, he took her right nipple between his teeth, not biting, just holding, and then he licked and sucked until she was squirming and pulling his hair a lot harder.

He stopped but only long enough to torment her left nipple in the same dastardly fashion. The only thing she could do was wrap her legs around his waist and ride it out.

By the time he'd moved down, she was ready. As much as she loved the whole foreplay thing, that wasn't what she wanted now. She pushed herself up by her elbows, and that got his attention.

"What?" he whispered, his voice as thick and low as his tongue.

"Please," she said. "I want you in me."

He didn't move for a long moment, and she thought he was going to ignore her, especially when he bent his head. But all he did was kiss the top of her mound, then the top of each thigh. He rose up, so tall, his shoulders so wide and strong. His hands brushed her sides, moving slowly upward until he had to brace himself or fall.

She'd never wanted like this before. Not with the boy she'd thought she'd loved in college, not with the men she'd hoped would become the one. She opened herself to Boone, and when he pushed himself inside her, she felt something shift. She couldn't have said where, except it was awfully close to her heart.

She folded herself around his body and wished again that she could see his eyes. In the end, it didn't matter. She knew who he was. And she knew who she was with him.

13

WHEN SHE GOT UP THE NEXT TIME, she was alone in the bed. Boone was gone, and her heart sank, missing him. She listened, but she didn't hear talking, or walking, or Milo, and she was instantly afraid.

After pulling on her clothes, she padded to the door in Boone's socks, opening it slowly. No one was in the living room. Had she dreamt that Seth and Kate had spent the night? Listening again, she still heard nothing. Even though she really needed to use the bathroom, there was no way until she found out what was going on.

Where was Boone? Maybe he'd taken Milo out? She hoped that was it, but since nothing good had happened in such a long time, she didn't count on it.

Quietly, she went through the living room, scoping it out. No bags, no clothes, nothing that said Seth and Kate were there or ever had been.

The kitchen was empty, too. But there was a note on the table and the coffee was almost finished dripping. Christie let out a breath as she picked up the note. Okay. Boone had Milo, and they were just out front. Which was good, because it occurred to her that she had forgotten the gun.

It was no contest what she had to do next, and it had nothing to do with a gun. In the bathroom, Boone had kindly left a brand-new toothbrush, which she used with his toothpaste. She needed a shower, but she had no clothes to change into. Not to mention the fact that she didn't want to risk being that vulnerable when Boone was out, even if he was just on his front lawn.

Retreating to the bedroom, she thought she could at least change socks. Maybe find a T-shirt that wouldn't be too big. Opening his top drawer, she found his boxers, which was kind of fun, especially the black silk ones, but no socks. Those were in the next drawer over. She grabbed a pair, and saw the edge of a picture underneath the rest. She pushed the socks aside, and her heart leapt to her throat.

It was a picture of Boone and Nate. Just the two of them. They were sitting on a bunk in an almost bare room. They had duffel bags by their feet, and light camo pants. They wore white T-shirts with their dog tags dangling from their necks. Nate had his arm around Boone, and they were both laughing. She'd never seen Boone look like that, not once. He was happy, goofing. Looking a lot younger, although she knew it wasn't that long ago, because Nate had his goatee. He'd only worn it for a short while, about two years ago.

They were in the Balkans. Where everything had gone to hell. This must have been taken pre-trouble.

Just looking at her brother and the man he'd sent to save her, made her knees tremble and tears come to her eyes. She missed him, goddammit. Missed him so much it made every part of her hurt.

"That was a damn good day."

She jumped at Boone's voice, and a second later, at Milo rubbing against her leg. "Don't do that."

"Sorry. I thought you heard the door."

Boone had showered. He looked awfully good in khaki pants and a gray T-shirt, with his hair a little damp, and he must have just shaved because his jaw was so smooth. She swallowed, remembering last night, how he'd made her quiver. She looked back at the picture, not wanting him to see the heat in her cheeks. "What were you laughing about?"

"It was stupid," he said, plucking the photo from her fingers. "As I recall, it had something to do with a redhead who had a very particular talent. Something you just don't see every day."

"I'm sure it was highly entertaining, but please, spare me the details."

"That's for the best. Now how about breakfast?"

"Great. I wish I had some shoes."

"We'll pick you up a pair on the way to the vet. We need to see that RFID."

"I just want it out of Milo," she said, following him to the kitchen. Halfway there, she remembered. "I'll be back in a second," she said, then turned and went to the bedroom. She picked up the gun, which was heavier than hers, made sure the safety was on, then put it in her waistband. By the time she got back to the kitchen, Boone had poured her coffee. She pulled out the cheese-cake herself.

"Is that what you're having for breakfast?"

"Yeah," she said. "So?"

"Lucky Charms weren't bad enough?"

"I'm a displaced person. Cheesecake is required."

He snorted as he went to an industrial-looking blender on his counter. He pulled out protein powder, two bananas, some yogurt, eggs, wheat germ, and some other things she couldn't readily identify.

She figured she was having cream cheese, strawberries, milk, eggs. All yummy and good for her. All she needed was a fork, and she was set.

Milo curled up under the table and snuffled happily. He didn't even blink when the blender whirred, having heard it so often at her house.

Christie dug in, and while she ate the absolute best food the planet had to offer, she thought about her brother. They'd had a weird childhood, the way most every childhood was weird. Dysfunctional mother, absent father, not enough money, too many upscale neighbors. But she and Nate had gotten along for most of it. He'd been wild, but in a very subversive way. He'd known in junior high that he wanted to join the army. That he wanted to fight, and win. So he had never gotten into trouble, even though he'd done a million things that should have gotten him kicked out of school, if not put in jail.

That's why it had been so hard to accept that he'd gotten himself into a situation he couldn't get out of. He wasn't supposed to die. He was the one who saved everyone else. He was the hero, who always got the girl.

"Hey, you're not shoveling that nasty stuff into your body."

"Yeah, well, suddenly I'm not so hungry."

Boone sat next to her, his giant shake in an equally giant glass in front of him. "What?"

"Just thinking about Nate. I still can't quite get that he's dead, you know? Like it has to be some kind of mistake. Nate was…"

"Invincible."

"Yeah. I saw him die. We'd had dinner, and he was really weird. He looked like hell, and he was jumpy and he wouldn't talk to me. I was so worried about him." She lifted her feet up onto the chair again, wrapping her arms around her knees. "I thought maybe he'd gotten into drugs or something. It was the only thing that made sense, even though it didn't."

"You were there?"

She nodded, wishing the memory wasn't so vivid. "The parking lot was almost empty. My car was near the restaurant, but he'd parked across the way. There weren't even any lights near his truck. I hated leaving him like that. I told him to come stay with me, but he wouldn't."

She took in a deep breath, and it was as if she could smell the scent of spices coming from the Thai restaurant. Feel the warm night air. "He hugged me goodbye, really hard. Told me he probably wouldn't be able to see me again for a long time. But that I shouldn't worry."

Boone scooted closer to her, but he didn't touch her.

"I got in the car, but I didn't start it right up. I was debating if I should try harder to get him to tell me what was going on. I watched him as he walked to his truck. I gave it up then. Right as he was getting inside. I decided he wasn't going to listen to me, so I might as well go home. I put my key in the ignition, and that's when the sky exploded.

"I was thrown to the passenger seat, and I hit my head. I think I was knocked out for a minute, but I'm not sure. All I know is that when I looked out of my shattered window, his truck was completely engulfed in flames. It burned so hot. The fire captain told me there had to have been an accelerant used, because the inside of the cab was almost completely melted. They found enough of him, though, so that I could bury him."

"Jesus, Christie. I had no idea."

She didn't say anything. Or even think much. Just tried to remember his face. The details, like his eyes, the way he smiled. "No one from the army came," she said, finally. "No one. We didn't even get a letter. Why is that?"

"I didn't know. Not until four months after. If I had, I would have come."

She shook her head. "I'm talking about the brass, Boone. His superior officers. The institution. He was the best soldier there was. I know it. He had medals. He was proud of what he did. So why weren't they proud of him?" She turned, then, and looked into Boone's green eyes.

"It wasn't the army. It was something else."

"What?"

He looked at the wall, then back at her, the internal debate written all over his face. Tell her? Lie? "There are groups in the government that have specialized interests. I'm sure you've heard of covert ops."

"Spy stuff."

"Right. One of these groups recruited us to do some

jobs. It was all politically dicey, and dangerous as hell. It didn't go as planned."

"You're telling me Nate screwed up?"

"No. None of us screwed up. We were sent to do something that turned out to be very wrong. When we refused to do it, this group wasn't…happy."

"This group. They're who killed Nate? Who are after you?"

He nodded. "I really don't want to tell you any more than that."

She leaned over so her shoulder was pressed against his. "Thank you. It helps."

"Yeah. I wish I could do more."

"You are. You're saving my life."

"You're Nate's sister. There was never any question."

She smiled, wanting so badly to kiss him. To drag him back to that awful bed and make long, slow love with him. Instead, she picked up her fork. The cheesecake was perfect.

BOONE CHECKED THE REARVIEW mirror yet again as he turned another corner. He'd studied his Culver City map before they'd left the firing range. He didn't take the freeway or any logical approach back to her house. No one was behind them. Christie hadn't said much, and the closer they got to her house, the more tense she became. She didn't want to go back, and he didn't blame her. Unfortunately, if she wanted her life back, there wasn't a good alternative. "You okay?" he asked.

"Milo's still sleeping," she said.

"The vet said he might do that, remember?"

She nodded. "Still…"

"I know. But he got a clean bill of health, so no worries."

"Right. No worries."

"Hey, you were great at the range. And you're going to be great once we get back to the house."

She turned to him, pale, tight. "I wasn't great at the range."

"You hit the target."

"The outside. Nowhere near his head or his heart."

He touched the hand on her thigh, and while she didn't pull away, she didn't return the gesture. "I trust you."

She sighed and looked out the passenger window.

"Talk to me," Boone said, pulling the car over to the side of the street. They were still a few blocks away from her place, but it wasn't far enough.

"I can't do this. I can't go back in there. He wins. He can have it, all of it. I just want to—"

"Who, hold on." He put the car in Park and turned to her. Behind them, Milo stirred and whined. "What happened? An hour ago you were ready to kick his slimy ass."

Christie wrapped her arms around her stomach. "I'm sorry. I keep thinking about that red dot on your chest."

"He won't kill me. He won't kill anyone."

"You don't know that. He keeps winning, Boone. I know you're trying. You're all trying, but—"

"The one thing that's true is that he can't stay away from you. And that's what we have to use."

"Me. As bait."

Boone hated this. Almost as much as she did. "That's about it."

"I could disappear. The world's a big place. I'm young and healthy. I could get work, start again."

"You're right. You could. You could leave everything you've ever known behind. I can even get you a whole new identity. Social security card, driver's license, all of it."

"Great."

"You could never speak to your parents again. None of your friends. Not even once, not even on their birthdays or if they have a baby. You couldn't go to a funeral. Or use your experience on a résumé. In fact, you shouldn't even go back into interior design, because he knows. He'd look. He'd keep looking. You'd never know when or if it was over. Never, because you don't know who he is. All you do know is that he's figured out every way to control your life. He's taken everything that matters to you. The last thing you have is your right to live *your* life. But you can give that to him, too, if you want."

She faced him, finally, and her eyes were so sad. "That's what it's like for you, isn't it?"

He nodded.

"How do you stand it?"

"I don't give up."

She gave him a little smile. "Okay. I won't, either."

"I won't let him have you. You know that, right?"

Her eyes closed for just a minute as she inhaled deeply. When she breathed again, she nodded, too. "I know."

Boone put the car in Drive and they went those last few blocks and pulled into her garage.

Seth and Kate met them as soon as they walked into

the house. This time, Christie remembered the gun, and she wielded it with a lot more confidence. It didn't go back into her purse, but into her waistband. Just like a real soldier.

She fed Milo, who seemed his old self, then met with the others at the kitchen table. Christie found herself searching for red laser dots, on the dog, on the wall, on Boone's chest.

"It's okay to talk here," Seth said, "but keep it down."

"You mean there are still bugs?"

"Yes. In the living room, the bedroom and the garage. They cover everything but the corners, so be careful in there. Don't say anything you don't want him to hear."

"I don't want him to hear anything. Get rid of them."

Boone looked as if he were going to pat her hand, but she backed away.

"I'm not kidding, Boone."

"I know. It sucks. It's impossible. But it's just for a little while. Until we get him in this house."

She put her head in her hands. "Fine. Do whatever."

"You just have to remember where it's safe," Kate said. "In here. In the bathroom and in the guest room."

"Oh, gee," Christie said, sitting back up, "that's swell."

"Look," Kate said, "we've got him covered. He can't make a move near this place without us knowing."

"Explain that, please."

Kate leaned a little over the table. She'd changed from last night's big sweater into a green button down shirt and black jeans, and her hair was loose and shiny. There was nothing girly in her eyes. "We wired everything. Including the perimeter. We replaced Boone's cameras with some new ones that are much more sensitive. They cover a lot more territory and they can pick up a whisper."

Christie nodded, thinking about the traps, but then it hit her. "Boone's cameras?" She turned to him. "What cameras?"

Boone got up a little too quickly and went over to the coffeepot.

"Boone?"

"The whole point to this operation is to catch this guy. It has been from the start."

"You put cameras in my house without telling me? It's not bad enough I have some sick freak out there spying on me?" She stood, so angry she wanted to throw the damn chair at him. She walked out of the kitchen, and the second she was in the hallway she realized that she was on camera. Whether it was Boone's or not, it was still filming her, still prying.

Had Boone seen her in her bedroom? Undressing? Had he watched her as she did something gross? Something she'd never want another person to see?

Turning on her heel, she went back to the kitchen. Boone was sitting with Seth and Kate, looking guilty as hell. "What about the bathroom?"

Boone shook his head. "It's fine."

"Is that the truth, or are you keeping it from me for my own good?"

"There are no cameras in the bathroom. There never have been."

She left them again, first going to the living room to get her clothes together, then down the hall. When she got to the bathroom, she slammed the door, wishing she had an air horn she could blow into the goddamn microphones.

Dropping her clothes on the counter, she sat down at the edge of the tub and tried not to cry. She was so sick of tears, sick of fighting tears, and sick of having no control over any part of her life.

Even the good guys were liars.

Screw it. She'd give them one more day. If they didn't catch the bastard, she was out of here. How much worse could running be? She'd find a new town, a waitress job. She'd sell her car and buy something old that ran. She'd even change her name, because this one wasn't doing a lot for her. As for not speaking to her parents again, they'd hardly miss her. Her money, yes, but not her.

She'd still have Milo. He was the only one she could trust, anyway.

The lavender bath oil seemed appropriate for steaming off fury, so she turned on the water and added a healthy dose. She'd soak until she pruned, and then she'd soak some more. The last thing she wanted to do was go outside again. Ever.

She'd trusted him. With her life. And now she wasn't sure what to believe. Better to assume it was all bullshit. All of it.

14

"OH, CRAP, BOONE," KATE SAID. "I should have kept my mouth shut."

Boone poured himself some more coffee, feeling like a total shit. "It's my fault. I should have just told her. I didn't think."

Seth was putting his equipment back into his bag, being his usual meticulous self. Everything in its place so he could retrieve it in an instant. "It's not as if you were trying to spy on her. You're just trying to catch this freak."

"I know, but she has a point. She's been terrorized by this asshole invading her privacy."

"Go talk to her." Kate came up to him and touched his shoulder. Not a usual move for Kate, so he knew he should pay attention. "We need to get it together for the next act, but I don't want to leave when she's so upset."

Boone turned to face his two comrades. "I don't know that she'll want to talk to me. If she kicks me out, I won't blame her."

"She's not going to kick anyone out. The woman still needs help, now more than ever." Kate got herself some coffee, and went back to sit with her papers. "I've got a few questions for her on some of these men. See if she's willing to talk, okay?"

"I'll do what I can." Boone reached into his pocket and pulled out the RFID that the vet had removed. He tossed it on the table, then headed down the hall. He knew Christie was in the bath, which wasn't the ideal conditions for a talk about privacy. He'd knock and see what her reaction was.

Not that he was any good in this kind of situation. Give him a room full of terrorists, and he was the man, but a single upset woman? That was enough to send him cowering in a corner. Hell he deserved a chewing out, and she deserved to give it to him. The last thing he wanted to do was hurt her more.

He stood at the door and tapped it quietly.

"What?" came the muffled voice from inside.

"It's me. Can I come in?"

"Why, you want to take pictures?"

He closed his eyes and leaned his forehead against the door. He thought about last night. How it had felt to be with her, to care about her. "No, I want to apologize."

"Great, thanks. That makes everything okay."

"Right, you're right. I was an idiot, and you get to be mad as hell."

"What?"

"I said—"

"Oh, just come in, for God's sake."

He tried the door, but it was locked. "I can't."

"You mean to tell me between the three of you, you can't jimmy a bathroom lock?"

"Hold on."

He went back to the kitchen and asked Seth to lend

him a hand. Boone knew how to get in using C4, but since that seemed a little much, he got Seth to use his handy kit. It took less then a minute, and Boone knocked once more before he opened the door.

Although his intentions were completely on the up-and-up, the moment he saw her naked in the tub, his body reacted. Even before the humidity got to him, he was sweating, and as he walked over to take a seat on the closed toilet, he felt the pressure in his jeans.

For her part, she just sat there watching him, her neck cradled in the pillow, the fragrant water holding up her breasts. Water droplets shimmered on her moist flesh, but she didn't take notice. She was too busy staring daggers at him.

"I was a jerk," he said.

"Go on."

"I should have thought, and I didn't. I was so focused on the job that I didn't take your feelings into account. I'm sorry."

Christie closed her eyes and let her head fall back. "Where are the cameras?"

"In the bedroom, the living room and the kitchen. I also have one on the front door and by the window in the guest room."

"So basically, everywhere."

"Yeah."

"Did you actually see him come into my bedroom?"

"I did."

"And?"

"There was no way to identify him. I got a general shape, size, but nothing concrete."

She looked at him again, and he squirmed under the glare. "Did it ever occur to you that I might be able to figure out who he is? That his shape and size would ring a bell?"

"No, it didn't."

"Okay, so we know that you shouldn't quit your day job to become a detective. Do you still have the tape?"

"Yeah. We'll take a look at it as soon as you're ready."

She didn't respond. She also didn't stop staring at him.

"I don't expect your forgiveness," he said. "You say the word, and I'm out of here. Seth and Kate will take over. They're damn good and they know the situation. You won't have to worry."

"You want to bail?"

"No."

"Then don't. But I swear to God, if you lie to me again, I'll use my new skills with my gun to shoot you where it hurts the most. Is that clear?"

"Crystal."

"Okay then. We'll look at the tape together. Then we'll get on with it."

"Fair enough."

"Do we have a plan?"

"We do. Seth and Kate are going to come back tonight, but they're going to put on a show for the geek."

"A show?"

Boone nodded. "They're going to tell us to get ready. To pack up for an indefinite period of time. We want the geek to believe we're going underground." He kept his eyes on her face, because every time they dipped below her neck, he forgot what he was saying.

"And this will do what?"

"Force the geek to come inside the house."

She sat up in the tub, revealing a lot more. "That's it? That's the whole plan?"

He focused. Again. "No. You're going to tell him that you don't care where you live because you and your boyfriend are going to be married. And then you're going to show him your engagement ring."

She looked at him for a long time. Finally, she sighed. "So where's this ring?"

He watched a single drop of water quiver on the tip of her nipple. "Ring?"

"I'm going to wave an engagement ring around?"

"Yeah."

"Boone, maybe I should get out of the tub and get dressed."

"No, don't."

"Pardon?"

He jerked his eyes up. "Sorry, what?"

She laughed. "Good to know that no matter what the uniform, boys will still be boys."

Boone stood, giving himself a mental whack on the head. He turned toward the door. It was just safer that way. "Okay, the ring. Yeah, we've got one. Kate brought it. Oh, and she wants to talk to you about a couple of men from your past."

"Which ones?"

"She didn't say. Were there any that were, you know, more than just casual relationships?"

"A couple."

"Really? Who?"

"Why," she asked, a smile in her voice, "jealous?"

"No, no. Just trying to figure this thing out."

Water sloshed, and he pictured her getting out of the tub. All that naked flesh dripping with warm, sweet water. He discreetly adjusted the boys, but it didn't help a whole lot. Then he tried to think of something really unsexy, but every image turned into naked Christie.

The water sounds stopped, but then he heard other stuff. A soft footfall, the towel slipping from the rod. "You probably want to get dressed," he said. "I'll go to the kitchen and wait."

"No, don't."

He turned to find her wrapped in her towel. Her hair was still tumbled atop her head, and her skin still looked damp and warm.

"There's still some things to discuss. Aside from the plan, which I want to go over again. But this... I need to hear this from you. Alone."

Boone nodded. Whatever she asked, he had to give her the truth, as long as the truth wouldn't get her killed.

"I really appreciate what you told me about Nate, but I need more. I want to understand. What did he do that was so terrible someone had to blow him up with a bomb?"

"Christie..."

She sighed as she sat at the side of the tub. She reached down and pulled the plug, then dried her hand with the edge of the towel. "I don't give a shit about the danger. Been there, doing that. Just talk to me."

Boone walked over to the other side of the tub and sat down, angling himself so he wasn't looking at Christie. "We were recruited by a special ops group, an offshoot of the CIA who worked with the Pentagon. All of us were picked for our particular specialties. It was just good luck that Nate and I were both selected for the team. I'd also worked with Seth.

"Our assignment was in Pristina, Kosovo. We were to get to a rogue scientist working there. Destroy the lab, and everything in it, then get out."

"When you say 'get to' you mean kill, don't you."

"Yes."

"What went wrong?"

"Everything. The scientist wasn't who we were led to believe. The information we were told to destroy had nothing to do with terrorism. When we protested, this black ops group decided to clear up the misunderstanding by killing all of us, the scientist included."

"But—"

"Yeah. It surprised the hell out of us, too. And that's it. That's all I can say."

"So how is it going to end? With you dead? All of you?"

"No. We just have to get the truth to the right people. But the truth would have to include proof."

Christie didn't say anything for so long, Boone had to look. God, she seemed so sad. Not crying, but almost.

He went to her side and took her hand in his. "He was a hero. For real. He stood up for his principles, for what was right. You have to remember that."

She sniffed, then met his gaze. "Sounds like you were all heroes."

"Naw. Just grunts following orders. We were just smart enough to know who to take our orders from."

"Boone, is this plan going to work?"

"It's our best shot. If he thinks we're leaving, for good, he'll have to make a move. And he'll have to do it before Seth and Kate come back with the new identities, which gives us our window of opportunity."

"What if he decides to solve the problem like that special ops team did? By killing us both?"

"He wants you too badly for that," he said. "He may be insane, but he's not crazy."

Her lips quirked up. "Was that a compliment?"

"It was trying to be."

"I appreciate it. But I don't think you're right. I've read too many real-life stalker cases where the bad guy thought if he couldn't have the girl, no one could."

"We'll be ready for him. Whatever he does."

"We? As in you and me, or you, me, Kate and Seth?"

"The whole gang."

"Good. I'd hate to have our futures depending on my shooting skills."

"You could do it if you had to. But you won't. Trust me, we'll have it covered."

She stood up and went to the center of the room. She didn't move for a while, then she dropped her towel and reached for her panties.

He watched as she dressed herself. Panties—white and lacy, but not a thong, unfortunately—and then her bra. It was one of the most erotic things he'd ever seen. She wasn't trying to turn him on. The opposite was true, he thought. She was simply dressing, as she would if she were alone. Or with a longtime lover.

It hit him that this was a new experience for him. He'd seen a lot of women dress, but it was always after sex, or after a shower, and there was always a show of some kind, whether purposeful teasing or casual indifference. He knew and they knew it was all part of it. The post-game show.

This wasn't. Christie wasn't trying to get him to call the next day, or to touch her, or to notice her at all. She wasn't trying and she was the sexiest women he'd ever seen. Even with her slightly baggy jeans, and even when she sat on the toilet to pull on white crew socks. He was stunned at how badly he wanted her. That bit before when she was in the tub? Nothing. A twitch. This? This was a full-on body spasm, an electric shock. He wanted to make love to her all night long. He wanted to wake up to her the next morning, and see her hair a mess, and he wanted to see her yawn, and scratch and do all the things a person does when they aren't trying to be someone else.

"Boone?"

He stood up so fast he almost slipped on the rug.

She looked at him, puzzled. All her clothes were on. The jeans, the shirt, the sneakers. "Are you okay?"

"Yeah. Sure. Why don't you go on and meet with Kate. I'll be there in a minute."

"Oh, okay. Sure." She headed for the door, but paused before she opened it. "For what it's worth, I think the plan is a good one."

"We're a good team."

"Oh, and before I forget, thank you. For last night." She smiled at him, then left, closing the door behind her.

He sat down again, amazed at his incredibly horrible timing. He liked her. The woman was in a living nightmare, and he was thinking about asking her out on a date. Which was crazy, because the last thing she needed was him in her life. He wasn't just a wanted man, he was a marked man. They'd been running for too long for their luck to keep holding out. As soon as they caught the geek, Boone had to disappear again. He had to go back to his world of shadows and lies.

The worst thing he could wish on Christie, aside from the stalker, was to have anything at all to do with him.

KATE WAS AT THE KITCHEN TABLE with Seth. As soon as Christie walked in, Seth got up and went to the sink to rinse out his cup. Christie took the hint and sat down next to Kate. "You wanted to ask me some questions?"

"Yeah, thanks." She moved a picture over, one of a guy Christie had dated three years ago.

"What can you tell me about him?"

"Alan? He was a nice guy. Kind of unfocused. He kept trying different careers."

"Ah."

"What, that makes a difference?"

"Yeah, it does. A lot of stalkers have trouble maintaining jobs. They don't do well socially."

"That's not Alan. He fancied himself a renaissance man, but mainly he just got bored easily. He was a popular guy, went to a lot of parties."

"Okay," Kate said, pulling another picture out. "What about him?"

She almost didn't recognize the picture. "That's Ed, but when I knew him, he didn't have that much hair. Or the mustache."

"What was he like?"

"Nice. Really nice. The kind of guy you'd want to bring home to mother, if your mother wasn't mine. He loved chess and he was into Asian cooking. He made sushi a lot."

"What happened between you?"

"It was a long time ago."

Kate gave her a curious look. "I remember why I broke up with every guy I've ever been out with."

"Okay, yeah. He was too nice, okay? He wanted to please me so badly, it was like screwing an abandoned puppy. I couldn't take it."

"So you like it a little rough?"

"I didn't say that."

"Sorry. Didn't mean to step on any toes."

"What else do you need to know?"

Kate glanced at Seth, who didn't move one facial muscle, then back at Christie. "How was he socially?"

"He got along with people. He just wasn't real aggressive. He liked his cat. A lot. But he wasn't weird. Just nice."

"Okay. We won't cross him off the list just yet."

"There's no way in hell he got fiber-optic cable with pinpoint cameras. The guy had trouble setting up his VCR."

"Noted."

"Is there anyone you can think of who could do that? Who was particularly good with electronics?"

"Dan had a very high-tech home theater. But I don't think he set it up. But he did have an iPod, and a laptop. Used those a lot. On the other hand, so did most of the men I dated. Most every guy I know likes his toys."

Kate looked at Seth again. "True."

"Believe me, if I'd gotten any weird vibes from any of these guys, I'd say something. I would. But they're just guys."

Kate put the pictures back in the folder. "It's very possible this was someone you met casually. Someone you smiled at once, and never gave him another thought."

"That sure narrows down the field."

"Stalkers are sick. Yours just happens to be an electronics whiz. Did Boone tell you about the plan?"

"Yes, he did. He also said you had a ring?"

Kate nodded, then got her purse from the floor. She pulled out a small plastic baggie that held a diamond engagement ring. "It's real, so try not to lose it."

Christie took the bag and pulled the ring out. It was lovely. A nice-sized solitaire in a platinum setting. "Is there a story behind this?"

"Yeah, and there's not a chance in hell I'm telling it." Kate closed her purse.

"You sure you haven't dated any of those guys?" Christie asked, nodding at the file.

"Nope. Just carbon copies. I don't know where all the good ones are, but they sure keep their distance from me."

Christie sighed. "I hear you. They're all taken or gay, or good in the sack and nothing else."

"Good in the sack?" Kate opened the file. "Maybe I should date some of these guys."

It was nice to laugh, to sit back in her own kitchen with good people who wanted nothing but to help her. It was nice to have a moment that wasn't about terror.

BOONE STOOD IN THE HALL by the kitchen, wondering how long he should wait to walk in. Hearing Christie talk about the men in her life made his situation a lot less complicated. He was just another guy. Good in the sack but nothing else. He just wished knowing that didn't make him feel like hell.

15

CHRISTIE STEPPED INTO the safe zone in the kitchen, and signaled Boone to follow. Once he was there, she touched his arm. "What's wrong?"

"Nothing."

"Don't give me that. You've been sulking for the last two hours. Is there something wrong with the plan?"

"No," he said, as if she were the one who was being all weird.

"Then what the hell is it?"

"I told you," he said, looking at everything but her, "I'm fine."

"You're a liar. Somewhere between the bathroom and the kitchen, you went south, buddy. And since we're talking about luring a lunatic into my home tonight, it would be nice to focus on that instead of you. So get over yourself, or tell me what I did so that I can apologize."

"You didn't do a goddamn thing."

She sat down and put her head in her hands. Milo whined behind her, which was the perfect accompaniment. "Great. I've got the bastard watching my every move, a show to put on in under an hour, and now you're throwing a hissy fit."

When she finally looked up, Boone was glaring at her. She just glared right back. It was a game of chicken, and no way she was going to give in first.

"Oh, forget it," Boone said, turning his back to walk out of the room.

"What is your problem?" she called after him, not understanding at all. He'd been so sincere in his apology that she'd found her resentment completely overshadowed. So what on earth had gotten him so angry since then? Goddammit, his pissy attitude shouldn't matter at all. Her chest shouldn't hurt like this, her hands shouldn't be curled into useless fists. In fact, it was good to see this side of him. Here she'd been thinking he was this incredible guy, someone she could talk to, trust in, be herself with. She'd even thought that the two of them…

Was her judgment that off? Could she trust any of her feelings for him? Oh, screw it. She'd probably be dead by tonight, so what difference did it make?

BOONE HEADED INTO THE living room, but he couldn't stay there. The fucking geek was watching and if Boone couldn't kill him, he didn't want to think about him. Which left the kitchen, already occupied, and the bathroom, which was not a great place to hang out in, especially when there was nothing to punch.

Anything was better than the living room, so he went down the hall, stopped at the bathroom door, cursed himself for a fool, then went right back to the kitchen.

Christie was sitting where he left her, the anger in her expression softened not by forgiveness but by sadness. Which made him feel even more like shit.

"What?" she asked, looking up at him with her big, dark eyes expecting nothing.

"I—" He shut his mouth, wishing he'd thought this through before making his entrance.

"You...?"

"It's got nothing to do with you."

She shook her head at him. "It's just your time of the month?"

"Something like that."

"Right. You know what? Fine. Apology accepted. No harm, no foul. I'm hungry, and we don't have all that much time."

She stood up, pushed her chair into the table with enough force to let him know that it definitely wasn't fine.

Boone closed his eyes. The whole thing was nuts. So she didn't think that much of him, so what? This wasn't a popularity contest. He was here because he owed Nate, that's all. Because he wasn't about to walk out on her before they'd caught the geek. So they'd had sex. Big deal. It didn't mean anything. She didn't mean anything. Nothing. Sure he was attracted to her, so what?

He opened his eyes to find Christie holding a pint of Ben & Jerry's and a spoon. "What the hell's that?"

"Ice cream."

"You're not having that for dinner."

"Wanna bet?"

His anger rose again, filling him with heat and tension. "I'll make you something, okay? You don't have to lift a finger."

"Don't do me any favors," she said, tossing the lid in

the sink. She took a big spoonful of the chocolate ice cream and shoved it into her mouth.

"Goddammit," he said, crossing the room in three steps. "Don't you get it?" He pulled the container from her hand and shoved it into the trash can. "You're fighting for your life here. It's not a game. He wants to do you harm."

Christie turned halfway to the sink, then swung at him so hard and so fast, she blindsided him with a punch right to the jaw. It hurt like hell, too.

Her left arm came at him, but he snatched her wrist halfway to his face. "Ow."

"Let me go, you big oaf."

"No." He could feel her trembling with rage.

She pulled as hard as she could. "Let go. I'm not kidding."

"Not if you're going to hit me again."

"Eating ice cream isn't going to make a damn bit of difference," she said.

He dropped her hand and walked out of the kitchen. It was everything he could do not to put his fist through the wall.

CHRISTIE WRAPPED HER ARMS around her stomach, nausea making her breathe hard for a moment before she could even look at Boone. "I'm sorry. I don't want to screw this up."

"You won't."

"How do you know that? I can't even remember what I'm supposed to say."

He touched her shoulder, and she jumped. "Christie, look at me."

She met his gaze, fighting tears, fighting the urge to run until she couldn't run anymore. She felt terrible about how they'd left things, what she'd said.

"You are the strongest woman I've ever met. You've faced this thing for months, all on your own. Now we have a plan. A way to get your life back. We're not going to let this prick take everything from you." He looked at the front door, then back at her. "This is your home. It's your right to have your privacy. This man is scum, you understand me? And he might have some sophisticated equipment, but underneath all that, he's a coward. Nothing more. We can take him. We will take him."

She took another deep breath, this time letting it out slowly, focusing on Boone's eyes. She thought about that day at the supermarket, how that clerk had looked at him and turned white with fear. Boone hadn't even been trying. Then she thought about last night. He might not have the kind of feelings she wanted him to have, but he cared whether she lived or died.

He was a warrior, a fighter, and he was putting all his fierceness and his focus on one thing. All she had to do was trust him. Trust that his plan would work. That Seth and Kate knew exactly what to say and how to act. And she had to trust herself. That was the big *if*, wasn't it? Could she come through when it counted most?

"I believe in you," he said. "I believe in you the way I believed in Nate."

She sucked in a breath at the sincerity in his eyes, in his words. He meant that. He meant it from the heart, and dammit, she knew Boone Ferguson wasn't a liar. He'd spent his whole life fighting for the righteous cause, just like Nate. And if he thought she could play this part, maybe she'd better believe him.

"Christie?"

"Okay," she said. She sat up straight, put her shoulders back. "Let's lock and load."

"That's the ticket." He looked out the kitchen window one more time. "They're gonna be here any second. Remember, you're agreeing to all this because you're in love. You're going to be married."

She nodded, resisting the urge to touch him. He needed to concentrate on the bad guy. Only that.

IT WAS TOO WEIRD, KNOWING the bastard was listening. Watching as Boone opened the door for Seth and Kate.

Christie had watched the tape of the bastard in her bedroom, pouring that horrible syrup all over her bed, and she hadn't recognize him at all. Not on the first viewing or the fifth. She'd finally given it up, but now she wondered if she'd missed something.

"So what's the plan?" Boone asked, walking his friends to the living room.

"Look, we tried, but this guy's just not coming out. There's really only two options," Seth said, folding his arms over his chest. "Stay here and hope he makes a mistake, or get the hell out of Dodge."

"I know what I vote for," Christie said. "I have no interest in staying here. Not with him peering over my shoulder." She moved closer to Boone. "Especially not now." She held out her left hand, showing off the glittering diamond. "We're going to be married."

"Congratulations," Kate said.

"Thanks." Christie threaded her fingers through Boone's. "So, will he know? That we're leaving?"

Seth didn't answer right away. He looked around the house, then met her gaze. "We got his cameras. And his microphones. He may be watching, however, so you'll have to be damn careful you're not followed."

"We can be packed and out of here in an hour," Boone said.

"That would be great, except we won't have your papers until morning."

Boone cursed. "I don't want to be here a second longer than we have to."

"We'll be back by six," Seth said, his voice so serious Christie believed him completely. "Be ready to go. Leave everything that could identify you here. If I were you, I'd destroy your address books and reformat your computer. Don't take pictures or mementos. They'll only come back to haunt you."

"You don't think I'll be coming back?" she asked.

Seth shrugged. "I don't know." He pulled his wallet out of his pocket, and took out a card that he handed to Boone. Christie glanced at it and saw it wasn't a business card at all, but a note. She couldn't read it though.

Boone put his arm around her shoulder and led her to the kitchen. Seth and Kate joined them, all in the corner by the fridge. Once there, Seth's demeanor changed. He winked at Christie and clapped Boone on the back. "That RFID? It only had a half-mile range."

"Which means he's been close."

"Too close. Be careful."

"You think he'll come tonight, right?" Christie

asked, afraid even here where she knew there were no microphones.

"Yeah, we do."

"Let's get out there," Kate said. "I want to reiterate the wedding thing."

"Let's get it over with." Christie took Boone's hand and led the group back into camera range.

"Thank you again, you guys," she said. "It has to be expensive to get new identities."

"No sweat," Seth said. "And congratulations again on the wedding."

"I thought about waiting," Boone said. "But I'm not taking any more chances with her. No matter what, I want her safe. With me."

"We won't give up on finding him," Seth said.

Boone pulled her close. "Good. We'll pack it up and be ready to leave before six."

Seth held out his hand. "We'll see you then. Don't worry about it. By this time tomorrow, you'll have disappeared."

They walked to the door, and watched as Seth and Kate got into his truck. The whole thing had lasted twenty minutes, and everyone had played their part to perfection.

When Boone closed the door, he surprised her with a kiss. Not a fake one, either. She knew it was for the camera but she didn't care. He held her tightly, both tender and anxious, and she forgave him for being a jerk, because who wouldn't be with everything they had to face? By the time he let her go, she'd even forgiven herself.

"Let's get packing," he said.

She wished they really were leaving. That the ring on her finger wasn't borrowed. And as long as she was wishing, it would be great if her feelings for him were real, and if he truly did care.

BOONE WATCHED HER AS SHE folded clothes, putting them neatly into her large suitcase. She was all business, and she wasn't even terribly freaked out by being in the bedroom.

She really was remarkably strong. She'd held up better than most men would have, and he wondered again why there were no women allowed in Special Forces. Yeah, they went into dangerous situations, but the women he knew were amazing warriors. Kate had faced things no one should. Kosovo had been as tough as it gets, and all she'd been concerned about was saving lives and making sure justice was served. Not easy when corruption was the order of the day, and no one cared who died in the pursuit of power.

Then Harper and Tam, they'd nearly been killed too many times to think about. Not a whimper out of either of them. They just did what needed to get done efficiently and smartly. He was proud he'd gotten to serve with them, and it pissed him off royally that they were in hiding now, afraid for their lives, living in the shadows, like him.

And if they didn't catch the geek? He wouldn't wish his life on anyone, let alone Christie. It was lonely and difficult, and there wasn't a moment that went by that he wasn't aware he was hunted.

He'd thought a lot about the geek, and the possibility that he was connected to the Company. Just thinking about that made him angry, and he had to get up from the bed and walk off some steam.

Christie looked at him, but he just paced, waiting for her to get done with her business. Jesus, he wanted to get his hands on that prick. If he was connected, then there was no choice, they'd have to take him out. Then they'd have to find his place and clean it out. All that before going deep underground yet again. A new name, a new place to live.

He wished they could just leave L.A., but that wasn't possible, not if they wanted to ever get out of this mess. The men they were hunting had their headquarters here. The team had followed the evidence here, and this is where they'd get it back.

"Uh, Boone?"

He stopped. Christie stood a few feet away, concern all over her beautiful face. "Yeah?"

"You okay?"

"Yeah, I'm fine."

"Right. I'm done in here. I have to get Milo's stuff put together."

"Okay. I'll get your suitcase."

She watched him as he went to the closet, and he forced his thoughts to the here and now. Tonight might be the last time he ever saw her. If they were successful, and he had no doubt they would be, she would go back to her life, and he would go back to his. Maybe he'd figure out a way to check up on her. Make sure she was getting on all right.

No, that would be too difficult. He'd cut it off, make it quick. Say goodbye, and forget about her. When he was back in the world, that's when he'd find her again. If she were still available—

"Boone?"

"Yeah, right. Suitcase." He got the bag, in which she'd clearly packed bricks, and headed toward the living room. Christie followed until they reached the kitchen, where she went off to put together a bag of Milo's supplies.

Boone put the suitcase near the door, then went to the window. It was too soon for the geek to make his move, but he'd be listening. For the next few hours, they'd have to appear happy, confident that they'd be making a successful escape.

Nothing was happening on her street. No one was walking a dog or watering the lawn. It was almost nine, after the dinner hour. Time for TV or homework, or whatever happy families did on a weeknight.

"Is someone out there?"

He turned. Christie was standing in the light from the kitchen, her hair dark and shiny, her T-shirt snug across her breasts and loose in the middle where it hid her Glock. "No, nothing."

"I know it's going to hurt your puritan soul, but I'm going to make cookies. You can come and scowl at me if you want."

"Cookies? Again?"

"See? All's right with the world." She shook her head as she headed to the stove.

What the hell. Cookies, ice cream. She was right. Now was no time for denial. She could eat any damn thing she wanted tonight. Tomorrow, when it was over, he'd talk to her about her diet, and see if she'd be willing to make a few—

Shit. Tomorrow, he wouldn't say a word. She could eat cookies for dinner forever, it was none of his business. He went to the kitchen table and sat down. Milo came over for a pet, and Boone obliged.

He watched as she got out yet another package of frozen cookie dough, then turned on the oven. She wasn't shaking, or looking over her shoulder. In fact, she seemed remarkably calm. "Hey," he said, keeping his voice low now that they were in the safe zone.

"Yeah?"

"You okay?"

She came to the table and sat down next to him. "Shockingly, yes. It's going to go the way it's going to go. I can't do anything else to prepare, and I can't sit here and worry because that wouldn't do any good, either. So, it's cookies and hot chocolate. One step at a time. One foot in front of the other."

"Damn," he said.

Her lips quirked up on one side. "What does that mean?"

"It means I think you're pretty amazing."

"Yeah?"

He nodded.

She leaned over to brush her lips over his. "It's mutual," she whispered.

He held her steady with both hands and kissed her, hard. He hoped like hell it wasn't their last.

THEY FINALLY GOT INTO BED at two. Of course, neither of them would sleep, but they had to keep quiet as well as stay alert. Christie had managed to feed him a half-dozen cookies, and he felt weighed down, even though he knew he was imagining things. Before a battle he liked to feel hungry.

The only thing he was hungry for was more time with her. Now that it was all coming to a close, he felt as if it had gone by in a flash. Forgetting her would take a hell of a lot longer.

Dressed and with her weapon snug in the waistband of her jeans, she crawled into bed and pulled the covers over her body. He got in next and once he was settled, he listened carefully, but there was only the soft sound of her breathing to break the early morning silence.

The worst part of the evening had been taking Milo out. They'd let him run in the backyard, both of them watching, and waited while he found the perfect spot to do his business. The whole time Boone been incredibly aware of Christie's fear. She hadn't said anything, but man, the vibes pouring off her were palpable.

He'd comforted her as much as he could, but in the end the only thing that had helped was coming back inside. Of course, that was where the real danger lay. If the geek was going to make his move, it would be sometime in the next few hours. Had it been Boone's operation, he wouldn't wait too long. The best time would be when the targets were in the REM cycle, about forty-five minutes after they'd first fallen asleep.

He stiffened as he felt Christie move, but realized quickly that she'd simply touched his side with her fingers. He found her hand with his and gave her a squeeze. What he wanted to do was hold her, but he couldn't take the chance. They had to mimic sleep, get their breathing slow and steady. Holding Christie would make that impossible.

"I can't stand this," she whispered, so softly he just made out the words.

"Yes, you can. Just breathe deeply, visualize shooting the target. Go through every motion carefully and slowly."

She tugged at his fingers and he heard her take in a long breath.

He, on the other hand, didn't think at all about shooting, but about who it was that had done this to Christie. His vote was for an ex-boyfriend, someone she'd let go. He could understand being upset about that. Christie wasn't your average woman, and for a man to find he didn't measure up would be a real blow. The road from hurt to obsession wasn't long. Given time, desire had morphed into the need for revenge, coloring his whole existence.

And that made this plan the right plan. This man, this sick bastard, wouldn't be able to stand the idea of someone else taking "his" Christie away. He'd have to do something tonight, before she could be stolen. But how would he get into the house?

The last time, he'd cut open a window. If he did the same tonight, Boone would know it before he finished the first cut. Seth had put sensors on every windowpane in the place including the bathroom, even though the geek would have to be a child's size to get in there.

If the geek were smart, and he was, he'd try another route. The garage, perhaps. There was only the one door which was locked, but not with a dead bolt. It wouldn't be that difficult to jimmy the lock, and get in the house. The disadvantage there was his lack of a camera or microphone. He couldn't know if someone was lying in wait.

He wouldn't try the front door. The dead bolt, the likelihood of being spotted by a neighbor. The risks were too great. Which left what?

Milo whined, got up, turned in a circle, then lay down in the exact same spot next to the bed. His head went to his paws, then lifted again, looked about, then down. Boone supposed he was feeling Christie's anxiety, but didn't know what to do about it. He could just reach far enough to give the old boy a pet.

His hand went over Milo's head and neck, and the dog snuffled his appreciation. Boone didn't mind the contact, either. His thoughts turned back to the geek as he let his hand roam idly down Milo's flank as he eliminated one entry way then another. His finger brushed against something that stopped him cold.

He touched it again. A dart. "Oh, shit," he said, throwing off the cover and bringing up his gun.

"Too late, Boone. Why don't you just put that down on the floor before I put my bullet through your brain."

16

CHRISTIE FROZE, terror swallowing her whole. He was here. In her house. Afraid to move at all, she did shift her head enough that she could see the end of the hallway. All she could make out was a dark shape, nothing clear, and not enough to figure out who he was.

"All right," Boone said, in the voice he used to calm her down. "Just cool it. I'm putting down the gun."

How could this bastard tell that Boone had a gun? Night vision, like in the cameras. Shit, he could see them, but they couldn't see him. And how had he gotten in?

"Slowly," the bastard said. "Try anything tricky and I'll kill you."

"All right."

Christie heard a thump as Boone's gun hit the carpet. Now that she'd heard the voice a second time, there was something familiar about it, but she couldn't connect it to anyone she knew.

"Now get up. Both of you."

Boone squeezed her hand quickly, then started to rise to his knees. She knew the bastard meant business, but she couldn't move. If she kept breathing like she was, she was going to hyperventilate again, and God knows what he'd do to Boone. She longed for her baseball bat, but she had no idea where that was. The gun in her waistband should have been a comfort but she couldn't figure out how to get it out and aim and shoot when she couldn't even see him.

"You, too, Christie. On your feet."

"Why are you doing this?" she asked, ashamed at how her voice trembled.

"Just get up."

She tried to move—honestly, she did—but her legs were stiff and the pressure on her chest was too heavy. Bracing herself on the mattress, she pushed herself up and then she remembered the flashlight.

How could she get it when her heart was beating so hard she could feel it in her toes? She wanted to be brave, to save the day, to be Sigourney Weaver facing the alien. But she couldn't even get her hand to move to the side of the mattress.

It was right there.

"You want me to shoot him? Is that what you want, Christie?"

"No," she said. "I'm just scared, okay? So it's hard."

"Scared? You don't know scared."

Boone got to his feet, keeping his hands in the air. "I'm going to help her, okay? One hand down."

"No. She can do it herself."

It sounded as if he were closer. He'd moved a couple of feet, she thought. More in the living room than in the hall. She took a deep breath, and as she let it out, she moved her left hand those few inches beside the mattress. Her fingers touched the cold metal of the flashlight, and she gripped it so tightly she could feel the switch dig into her skin.

"You," the bastard said. "Move away. Get off the mattress."

"Sure," Boone said. "Whatever you say."

The bastard laughed. "You think that's going to work on me? You moron. I've seen it all. Everything. You think you found all the cameras?"

"No, I'm sure we didn't."

"Just shut up. I don't want to hear another word from you. Christie, stop stalling. Do it."

Boone was now farther away from her, but she could at least see him in the hazy light coming through her curtains. It was more difficult to see where the bastard was, as the hallway was so far from the window. There was nothing to do but try. It would have to be quick and sure, and she was neither.

But Boone was counting on her. There was no doubt in her mind that the bastard would shoot to kill.

She pulled her legs under her, balanced on her right hand. The flashlight was under the edge of the blanket, so she knew the bastard couldn't see it.

"What do you want from her?" Boone asked.

"What did I say? Did I tell you to shut up?" The bastard's voice had risen to a shout.

"What did she do to you?"

"Boone," she said, "shut up."

"I just—"

"Shut up," she said, louder this time. Everything would be over if the bastard turned away. She had to keep him looking at her, watching her. "I know what he wants. And I'm going to give it to him."

The bastard laughed, and the sound made her sick to her stomach. It was as if all his twisted desires were right there in that low laugh.

She held her breath as she got to her feet, holding the flashlight by her side, making sure her finger was on the switch. "Tell me what you want," she said, needing his voice to get her bearings. "I'll do whatever you say."

"I know you will. You'll do every single—"

She turned on the switch at the same time she pointed the light straight at his voice.

He yelped, and then she heard a crash. Boone was on him, and they were both on the floor, the bastard's gun glinting in the beam.

"Your gun," Boone screamed, and then he took a blow that knocked him to the side.

She ripped at her T-shirt and got the Glock. She was holding the flashlight and she didn't want to drop it, but she'd never fired the gun with one hand.

The two men were still on the floor and she'd never been so scared in her whole life. If that prick hurt Boone, she'd kill him a hundred times.

Their grunts and punches sounded flat and unreal. If she could just get the gun over to Boone, it would all be okay. She tried to steady the light, but when she did, she saw that the bastard was hitting Boone with the butt of his weapon, and Boone was bleeding badly. He punched the son of a bitch, but it only stopped the fight for a moment. The gun came up again, smashing against Boone's temple.

She couldn't aim the gun, not when she was shaking

so hard. Boone's words came back to her, telling her what to do.

She climbed over the mattress and didn't let herself think, she just went to where he was bashing Boone with the gun and she had to stop him, right now. She threw the flashlight down, held her gun with both hands and pushed it into the bastard's side, right there, right where he was lifting his arm to hit Boone again, and then she closed her eyes and pulled the trigger.

Nothing happened.

It was the safety. She cursed and slipped the safety off, but then her legs were knocked from under her and she fell so hard her head bounced off the carpet and she couldn't see or feel anything but pain.

The gun, her gun, was ripped out of her hands, and she curled up into a ball waiting to feel the bullet rip through her body. The sound of the gunshot made her scream and she jerked, but she didn't feel anything except the pain in her head. All she could think was that Boone had to be okay. He had to or she would die.

"Christie."

Hands on her shoulder, shaking her and she couldn't open her eyes or stop the scream that was building in her throat.

"Christie, I've got you."

She gasped as she opened her eyes. It was Boone, standing above her, swaying back and forth.

He lurched away to the hall, and the light blinded her painfully. When she looked up again, Boone was leaning against the wall, his face bloody, his right eye swollen. Her gun was in his hand, and dripping.

She struggled up and went to him, needing to make sure he was really there, that they were both still alive. She touched his shoulders then pressed herself against him, and when he looked down at her, that's when she cried. Her tears flowed as she looked at his bruised and bloody face.

"Are you okay?" he asked.

"No," she said. Then she rose up on her toes and kissed him.

He grunted, but he kissed her back.

She tasted his blood, but she didn't care. They'd made it. They'd lived. She was in Boone's arms.

When she finally pulled back, she caught his wince. His mouth was really banged up, his lip split at the corner. "Oh, God, you're really hurt."

"I'll be fine," he said. He nodded past her. "You recognize him?"

She forced herself to look at the body lying on her carpet. "Oh, God."

"Who is it?"

"Dan. The guy I... It's Dan."

"He won't be—"

The front door flew open and Seth ran in, weapon drawn, his face a mask of rage. It took a moment for him to register that it was already over, and even then he went to the body, and kicked away Dan's gun, then checked his pulse. As he crouched there on the carpet, he looked at the two of them. "Sorry. He didn't trip any of the alarms. We didn't know until we heard him talking."

"I don't know how the hell he got in," Boone said. He closed his eyes. "I'm thinking crawl space."

Seth came over to her and touched her shoulder. "You okay?"

"We've got to get Boone to a hospital. And call the police."

"We can't call the police," Seth said. "And I've got a first-aid kit in the truck."

"What are you talking about? He's dead. We have to call the cops."

Seth shot a look at Boone. "He wasn't just a stalker. He couldn't be, not with his equipment. We need time to check it out. And we won't get that time if the police are called in."

"You think he's a spy? That makes no sense. What could a spy want with me?"

"We don't know," Seth said. "That's what we need to find out. Now let me go get the first-aid kit, and you take care of Boone."

"I'll be okay," Boone said. "Seth, have you called Harper?"

"Yeah. I'll be right back." He left, closing the front door behind him.

Christie stared at the closed door for a moment, still trying to process that Dan, who'd seemed so very normal, had been the one who'd destroyed her life. She didn't believe it about him being a spy. He had a practice. She'd been to his office, and there had been real patients there. If this was about Nate, it still didn't make sense. He hadn't told her anything. Ever. Her gaze went back to Dan's body, and she thought about that laugh of his. That wasn't about spies or Nate. He'd wanted to hurt her. Make her suffer.

The bastard had put cameras in her home to watch her in her most private moments. He'd gotten her fired from her job, had the IRS seize her accounts... She looked at Boone, who looked as if he might fall down any second. He didn't appear to have any life-threatening injuries, but God, he looked awful. "I don't understand," she said. "How did Dan get the IRS to do what he wanted?"

Boone shook his head, although the movement was tentative. "I don't know. But we're going to find out."

She nodded, but her thoughts had turned to Milo, who was so still. She went over to him and touched his head, terrified. He was warm, and better than that, he opened his eyes a bit. As she ran her hands down his flank, she found the dart and pulled it out of him. He didn't even whimper. "What did he do to you, sweetie? My poor baby."

Boone turned on the living room light so she could look at Milo more carefully. He didn't seem too bad, just lethargic, but she wouldn't believe he was okay until he was checked out by the vet. She stroked him over and over, her anger and confusion so overwhelming that she started shaking again. "Please be okay," she whispered. "Please."

Seth came back in, this time with Kate. He carried a large black bag, and Kate had something gray and bulky in her arms. They were both dressed in dark clothes and Kate had her hair tied back. Seth put down his bag then checked out the nasty cut on Boone's forehead. "You'll live," he said. "We need the keys to her car."

Boone had them from their last foray outside, and he handed them over. "That's Dan," he said. "The psychologist."

Seth looked at the body. Jesus, the dead body. Christie sat back on her heels, the enormity of what they'd done hitting her like a brick.

"We'll find out everything we can," Seth said. "Check out his house, find his car." He went over to Dan and without hesitation explored his pockets, retrieving a key chain and wallet. "Christie, why don't you take Boone into the kitchen and clean him up."

She stood on shaky legs and headed for the kitchen, not looking down, trying not to think about what Seth was going to do with Dan's body.

Boone brought the big black bag with him and put it on the kitchen table. When Christie sat down, she studied his face and saw that there were only two gashes. They'd bled a lot, but neither of them were bad enough to need stitches. The bruises were a lot more severe. His eye was already turning colors and so was his left cheek and the side of his mouth.

She got up, touched Boone on the shoulder as she went to the sink. She got a couple of clean dishcloths, wet and soaped one, then went back to him. He watched her with his good eye and submitted quietly to her ministrations, only hissing once when she cleaned the worst of the cuts.

After he was clean, she got out some bandages, studiously avoiding the scene in her living room. "Boone, how can we not go to the police?"

"It's going to take us at least twenty-four hours to check out this guy. If the police are called, they'll send someone to his house, and they won't wait for us to finish. And there's no way we can hold the body until we're through. Trust me. It's for your protection, too."

"Someone's going to miss him."

"Most likely, but they won't connect him to you. Seth will make sure of that."

"I hate this. I hate that I knew him. That I dated him. I don't understand why."

"We'll figure it out, okay? But you have to trust us."

"I do," she said, carefully pasting a butterfly bandage to his forehead. "I trust you." She examined her work, and decided all he needed now was ice for the bruises. "You know, I thought I'd be relived," she said. "I'm not."

"You will be. We'll go see my hacker friend, Larry, as soon as it's light. By the time we get back, the house will be yours again. No cameras, no microphones. Nothing at all to remind you of him."

Seth came through the kitchen and went into the garage. A few seconds later, she heard her car start up. Of course. He'd have to remove the body in secret.

When she looked to the living room, she saw that Kate's bundle had actually been a body bag. Dan was inside it, in the hallway. Her carpet was matted with his blood, already turning a sickly brown. She thought about what he'd done to her bed, and her anger rose again. There was no doubt at all that they'd killed him in self-defense. If she had remembered to unlock the safety, she would have shot him herself. The man was evil, and he deserved what he got. It didn't make it easier not to call the police, but if Boone said they couldn't, then she'd sign on.

He'd saved her, and almost gotten himself killed in the process. He'd involved his friends, putting them all at risk. How could she ask him, any of them, to do more?

She thought about her brother, and how much these

people must have cared for him to do this for her. Wherever he was, she hoped he was proud, and as grateful as she was.

"Stay here, okay?" Boone said. He went to the living room, where Seth waited. She hadn't even heard him walk back from the garage. Kate was with them, but when Christie glanced into the kitchen, she headed toward the table.

"Hey, you all right?"

"I think so."

Kate sat down. She looked tired and anxious. Christie had the feeling this was harder for her than it was for Boone and Seth. Kate wasn't a soldier. She'd clearly been involved in some horrible things, but the guys, they were used to all this covert stuff, trained for it until it had become second nature. Kate had been with the UN, and there was no way covering up dead bodies was part of that protocol.

"We'll have to replace the carpet. We'll remove it now, and we'll have someone we can trust come in with a new one. You want the same thing?"

Christie sat back in her chair, laughter bubbling from somewhere deep. Carpet choices? Now? "Yeah, the same carpet will be fine."

"Great. It'll all be over soon. You'll have your life back. That's gotta feel good."

"I don't believe it. Not yet."

"Sure," Kate said. "That's understandable."

Christie leaned a little closer to her as the men carried the body bag through her kitchen. "Do you really think he was a spy?"

Kate shrugged. "Best to cross all the t's and dot the i's. None of us can afford to leave it like this. But for what it's worth, I think he was obsessed with you. I heard him, and even over the speakers, there was a lot of twisted passion in his voice."

"Yeah. I heard it, too."

"There's no way this was anything but self-defense. You're not getting away with murder. Got that? You did good, and with any luck at all, you'll be able to put all this behind you."

Christie leaned back on her chair, suddenly so tired she could hardly hold her head upright.

"Why don't you get some rest? We'll take care of things out here."

"Milo."

"We've got it covered." Kate stood up. "He's going to be fine. And so are you."

Christie wanted to believe her.

17

BOONE STOOD BY HER BED, watching Christie sleep. He'd swallowed a couple of aspirin, which had taken the edge off, but he still hurt, though not as much as looking at her. Christ, her mouth was open, her hair was a mess and she looked too pale and thin to deny the stress she'd been under, but he thought she was the most beautiful woman he'd ever seen.

This was it. Yeah, they still had to find out about her bank accounts, and make sure there were no complications over at the prick's house, but it was over. He'd be leaving, going back to the business of scraping out a living and doing his damnedest to out those bastards who'd tried to kill the team. Before this, before Christie, taking them down was all he cared about. Now he just wished he'd never been in the service at all.

Other men could look back at a woman as the great heartbreak of their life. For Boone, it was the army. He'd given the service his heart, his soul, his body. And it had betrayed him in every way a man can be betrayed.

Until he'd gone to Kosovo, he'd had an exemplary record. Delta had recruited him, and they'd competed with the SEALs to win him. He and Nate had gone head-to-head, and they'd kicked everyone else's ass. It had been great.

It had gone to hell so quickly. One assignment. It had looked like a cakewalk up front. Then they'd met Tam, and she'd shown them exactly who they were working for. A government agency that was unconnected to the army or Delta Force, funded as an offshoot of the CIA. They had no compunction about breaking the law, about subverting the principles of the Constitution or international treaties. They'd turned Nate's unit into assassins for profit, and lied with every word out of their corrupt mouths.

The moment of discovery had been their last free moment.

Boone had gone home, met his father in secret, hoping for counsel, for support. His dad, the Major, had slapped him across the face and told him not to come home again.

Since then, he'd lived every day as if it would be his last, and not particularly cared. Yeah, he wanted justice, but mostly he wanted to rest. He wanted to get a regular job, maybe doing some high-tech security, maybe open a store in a quiet part of Tennessee.

Mostly, though, he wanted Christie. If things were different, he'd like to take her to his hometown, show her around. She'd like it there, in the mountains. So would Milo. That dog wouldn't know what to do when he saw some of those homegrown squirrels.

Christie shifted on the bed, her arm moving closer to her pillow. It ached, wanting her. Knowing that it might be years before he could come out of hiding. That it might be forever.

Just his luck he'd finally found someone he could love, when there was no hope of doing a damn thing about it.

"Hey."

He smiled at the soft, fuzzy voice, still half in sleep. "Hey, yourself."

"What time is it?"

"Almost eight."

"In the morning, right?"

He nodded. "There's someone here who wants to see you."

She sniffed and fought a yawn. "Can it wait till I brush my teeth?"

"I don't think he cares." Boone turned and patted his leg. Milo, tail wagging hard, came down the hall, his nails clacking on the hardwood.

Christie sat up, her smile so beautiful it made Boone's chest hurt, and when Milo jumped onto the bed, she hugged him so hard he almost fell right back down again.

Boone had to leave, to turn away from her. She'd come on out when she was ready, and they'd take off. He'd called Larry to find out where he was with the IRS business, but he'd only gotten the machine. Seth was going to stop by later, after they'd finished their search at Dan Paterson's house.

Kate had called an hour ago. Dan's place was a suburban one-story in Santa Monica, and the preliminary search hadn't turned up squat. No electronics, no mention of Christie, nothing. They'd all agreed that made no sense, so they were digging deeper.

As he passed the living room, his gaze went to the

bare patch Seth had cut out of the carpet. If they couldn't make the replacement seamless, they'd take out the whole damn thing and put in a new one. That wouldn't happen until tomorrow, though. First things first, but damn, Boone wanted to get Christie back to her rightful life as soon as possible.

Already, they'd removed most of the surveillance equipment. He wanted Seth to go through the house again, though, to make sure nothing was left behind. Then he wanted to change her locks and replace the bedroom window. They'd found the crawl space, where Dan had waited to spring his trap. He'd had earphones and a small monitor down there, which Seth had taken with him. Before he'd left, they'd nailed the access doors shut both inside and outside the house.

Everything was coming together, and once her finances were back in order, she'd be fine. She could work again, have her friends back in her life, see her parents. Her nightmare would be over.

"Boone?"

He turned to see her standing by the bathroom door, holding a bundle of clean clothes. "Yeah?"

"How about whipping me up one of your wonder shakes for breakfast."

He grinned. "No cookies? No ice cream?"

She wrinkled her nose. "Perish the thought. And double up on that wheat germ, would you?" She laughed as she closed the door behind her.

His smile faded as he went into the kitchen. For the thousandth time, he cursed the bastards who'd stolen his life, and swore, once more, that he'd have his revenge.

CHRISTIE STOOD IN THE SHOWER with the water hitting her in all the right places. She should have felt great. So much had gone right last night. Yeah, finding out the bastard was Dan was disturbing on a lot of levels, but the bottom line was, it was over. No more hiding in the corners. No more terror at the sound of a ringing phone. But…

No more Boone.

She hadn't known him long enough to feel this crappy about losing him.

He was going to leave, and she was going to have… what? Yeah, her life back. Hopefully her money back. No job, but that was okay, because she could get another job. A better job. And she'd have her friends again. So, yes, it would all be good. Great. Empty.

Maybe it was for the best. Clearly her choice in men sucked. When she thought about Dan… Jesus. As she washed her hair, she considered her relationship with him. He hadn't seemed weird. In fact, he'd seemed really normal, except for all the questions. That should have tipped her off, right? Him wanting to know everything about her family, about her work? But he was a psychologist, for God's sake. It made no sense.

She didn't want to think about it anymore. What she needed most was to sleep for a month, to gain back her strength and her perspective.

WHEN SHE GOT TO THE KITCHEN, Boone was at the table staring at the wall, holding a big tumbler of breakfast smoothie and idly playing with Milo. Aside from his ugly bruises, which ironically, made him look even more ruggedly handsome, he seemed deflated. As if now that the thrill of the hunt was over, he had no rudder, no purpose. She understood that, a little more acutely than she wished.

It was anticlimactic in a way. All this focus on catching a demon, and he'd turned out to be an asshole in a demon suit. Despite the truth, she still had a hard time associating the Dan she'd dated with the stalker. The cruelty was so much larger than the man. He'd delighted in her torment. A man who'd purportedly helped people get over pain and suffering.

She'd have preferred sending him away to prison, if not a psychiatric hospital, but he'd taken away their choice. It would take time for her to recover from the entire ordeal, and, she realized, it would take Big, Bad Delta-Force Guy a while, too.

Although she'd have sworn she didn't have a nurturing bone in her body, seeing him so sad and so banged-up made her want to cook him chicken soup and put him to bed. She had no chicken, so that was out. But the bed part? That had possibilities. One more for the road. A last goodbye.

Oh, that made her chest hurt. Despite his tendency to be a pain in the ass, having Boone around had been illuminating. And not just the sex. He thought she was strong. Capable. A fighter. No one had ever told her that before. She'd been her only cheering section when it came to facing the hard stuff. But these last few days, Boone had been her champion. She flushed at the thought, but it was true.

"You gonna stand there and stare at me, or come drink your breakfast?"

"You can't truly be snarky when you're talking about a health drink, you know."

"I can be snarky about anything."

To Milo's delight, she joined them at the table, petting him lavishly for surviving yet another tranquilizing episode. Boone seemed pleased, too, although his smile was crooked from the swelling.

She drank some of her drink, surprised yet again that it didn't taste like swill. When she put it down, she pushed back her still-damp hair. "So, we go to see the hacker guy now?"

Boone shook his head. "He's not home. Seth is gonna stop by later today."

"Which leaves us with what?"

"We should replace that bedroom window. And do another sweep of the house for bugs."

"Ah, another typical, what is it, Tuesday?"

His head quirked to the side. "I don't know."

"Weird, huh? It feels like we've been in an alternate universe."

"Actually, it hasn't been all that different from the rest of my life. Better company, but that's about it."

"Oh, God. I didn't think. I'm sorry."

"Not your fault. I'm just grateful that you don't have to go through it anymore. What are you going to do about work?"

"It depends on the cash situation. I still have to pay the mortgage, you know?"

"If anyone can get the IRS off your back, it's Larry.

I still want to know how the doctor had the connections in the first place."

"You think he wasn't really a psychologist, don't you?"

"I don't think that's all he was."

She drank some more, and so did he. Across the street, a gardener mowed the lawn. For the first time in ages, Christie opened the blinds all the way. She saw her own sadly neglected front yard, her mailbox—which she hadn't checked in too long—the sky, clouds. It all seemed so normal, so prosaic. And Boone couldn't have any of it. "Why do you stay?" she asked, turning to him. "Why not leave the country? Get a new name, a new start?"

"They stole my life from me. I can't let that go."

"They have money and power and resources you can't possibly match. I admire your principles, but how are you going to get them?"

"We just have to get the right kind of proof, and get it to the right people."

"You make it sound so simple."

"It is simple. It's just not easy."

She nodded. "I don't have any way of saying thank you."

"Sure you do," he said, smiling that crooked smile. "You just did."

"Cute. But not close. You saved my life."

"Actually, you saved mine. That flashlight move was downright brilliant."

She sat back, awash with pride. "Wow, it was, wasn't it?"

"Yep. You were magnificent."

Her cheeks heated, but not entirely because of his compliment. "I didn't take the safety off."

He shrugged. "It all worked out in the end."

"I suppose so. I'm almost afraid to ask, but what did Seth do with him?"

"Better you don't know."

"Yeah, I guess."

"Don't think about that," he said. "We did what we had to do. You're safe now, and that's what's important."

She got up, not sure what to do with herself. Her gaze fell on the missing carpet, but that upset her more. "Can we do something?" she asked. "Get that window maybe?"

"Sure." Boone got up and took both their glasses to the sink. He rinsed them out and put them in the drainer.

She looked him over, all the way up and down his long body. She liked him in those jeans. They were old and worn in a great way. No holes, just paler denim that covered that gorgeous butt to perfection. His shirt, also denim, did nice things to his back, to his wide expanse of shoulder. Altogether a wonderful package, but frankly, she liked him better without the wrapping.

"You want to grab your purse?"

"No," she said, walking over to him, wishing his mouth weren't so bruised. She touched his cheek as she studied his face. She'd remember him without the scars. Such a great face. Fabulous green eyes. Everything about him pleased her. Well, maybe not the way he shopped.

"What are you smiling about?"

She shrugged. "Happy thoughts."

"Good. You deserve happiness."

"So do you."

"I'm happy right now," he said, his hand slipping around her waist. "With you." He bent and kissed her.

She parted her lips, conscious of how gently they had to proceed. He was hurt, and she was aching at the thought of saying goodbye. So gentle was good.

He hissed once, then changed his angle, and his tongue had to do all the work. That was okay with her. They kissed like that, standing by the kitchen, until her shoulders relaxed and her limbs got wobbly. He ran his hands over her back and down, cupping her rear and pulling her tight where she felt him hard and thick.

A moan and a squeeze, and he stepped back. Again, that smile, that sad little bruised grin, and he took her hand to lead her down the hall, into the bedroom.

The undressing wasn't theatrical at all. Just hurried. He was naked first, all the way down to his long, elegant feet.

She still had her panties on, a sea foam green thong that cost more than a decent pair of shoes, which, from the look on his face, was worth every cent.

"Oh, my God," he said. He looked up into her eyes, and she saw such helplessness there, such bewildered loss.

"Boone, honey, what is it?" She closed in on him, not at all sure what was happening.

"You're so amazing."

She fought a smile because the way he said it was pained. "Thank you?"

He touched her hair. Petted her, actually, and then his splayed hand spanned her neck as he pulled her close. She nestled right in the crook of his neck, inhaling his warm scent, still unsure what had gotten him so upset. "Boone? Want to tell me what's wrong?"

He shook his head. She knew this because she felt his jaw touch the top of her head.

"Please?"

"You know that once we finish here, once the window is fixed and the money situation is straightened out, I have to leave."

"You live in Pasadena. It's not that far." She knew it wasn't that simple. That when he left, he would leave for good, but she couldn't... Not yet.

"Right," he said. "Pasadena. Nice town. Except on New Year's Day."

"You don't go to the parade?"

"I don't go to anything."

The hand that wasn't petting her hair was rubbing big circles on her back. It was the most soothing, wonderful feeling in the world. Meltingly sensuous, made more so by the contrast of his soft palm and calloused fingertips. He was right. It wasn't fair, not in any way. This man, he was something. The way she felt about him was so different from anything she'd experienced before. It was too fast, of course. No doubt about it at all. But it was true, nonetheless. He had touched her. Changed her. All she wanted in this life she had back was to know him better. To learn him.

"It's crap, Christie. What they've left us. It's not just me. There are five of us, and we don't go to things. We don't see our parents. We pay cash for everything, but that's not much because we might have to leave in the middle of the night with the clothes on our backs, so what's the point of buying things? We don't date, because wouldn't it be just our luck to have someone try to kill us over a nice prime rib."

"You'll stop them," she said, pulling back, meeting his eyes. Well, his one eye. "You will. But not today. Today, you're going to make love to me. For a long, long time. Then, we're going to finish the cookies, and make love again. Deal?"

He closed his eye and rested his forehead against hers. "Deal."

She pulled his hands down to the top of her thong. He took it from there.

18

EVENING HAD ARRIVED, and there was no more dodging the issue of getting out of bed. Poor Milo had been kept outside for most of the day, and he had to be lonely. But Christie didn't want to move, unless it was to turn over and snuggle closer to Boone.

His stomach grumbled, and that did it. She kicked the covers off and sat up. Damn, he looked great, all spread out and naked right there on her blue sheets. She stretched, feeling languid and a little sore, thinking about the shower. She should go by herself, because if they did it together, there was no guarantee they'd have dinner any time soon.

"Don't go," he said, then he winced and touched his lip.

"When's the last time you took an aspirin?"

"I don't need an aspirin."

"Oh, really? You feel no pain, is that it?"

"That's right, missy." He banged on his chest like a gorilla. "Real men don't need aspirin."

She bent over and kissed him, hard, on the lips. He yelped like a little boy. Still hovering inches above him, she smiled. "Liar."

"Okay, so we feel a little pain."

"I'm going to get out of this bed. First, I'll bring you medicine. Then, I'm taking a shower because, frankly, we're pretty rank. After that, I plan to eat an obscene amount of junk food. You may come with me, as long as you swear not to rag on me about my meal choices."

"I may, huh? I suppose I can hold back." He rolled over, nearly knocking her off the bed. "Wake me when it's time for food."

She slapped his naked butt. "Like hell. You get to feed Milo, you lucky stiff. And you get to shower as soon as I'm done."

"Hey, wait a minute."

"My house, my rules."

"But who's going to wash your back?"

"I'll manage. Now don't fall asleep." Christie got out of bed, wincing a little herself, and grabbed her robe from the back of her door. She went into the bathroom, got Boone some painkillers and a glass of water and made sure he took the pills. The she smiled as she gathered her clothes and headed for the shower.

THEY'D GONE FAST-FOOD ALL the way, including a plain burger without the bun for Milo, who was now frolicking happily on the grass while Christie ate and Boone scowled. He'd kept his promise and hadn't said a word. Not that he had to. The crease above his nose spoke volumes.

She looked around the park, enjoying the freedom of eating alfresco, even if it was at a picnic table. There were two other families sitting several tables away, and quite a few folks with dogs, which was why she'd chosen this particular park. Milo deserved a reward after all he'd been through. Just like she deserved the large order of fries and the chocolate milk shake. Boone, foolish boy, had gotten a grilled chicken salad with no dressing. Incomprehensible.

Just as Boone was about to say something, his cell rang, saving her, she felt sure, from a lecture on transfats. She half listened as he tried to tell Seth discretely why his phone had been off for most of the day, but mostly she watched Milo, who was fascinated by a Rottweiler's rear end. Boone's voice changed so dramatically that she forgot the dogs and zeroed in on the part of the conversation she could hear.

"When?" Boone asked.

She tried to catch his eye, but he was staring at the table, deeply focused and concerned.

"Get everything you can, and get out of there. The police could show up anytime."

Police? Christie pushed aside the last of her fries as she fell right back into fear mode.

"Good. Check back. Don't be long." Boone disconnected the call and looked up at Christie. "Larry's dead."

"The hacker?"

He nodded. "He's been dead for a while. We assume it was Dan's handiwork, but we can't be sure. Seth is collecting all the data he can, but the place was trashed so there's not much."

"Oh, God. Was he married? Kids?"

"He was divorced, no children. Goddammit, he was a good man. He didn't deserve that. Listen, we should get going. Lay low until we hear back from Seth."

She gathered their trash and tossed it while Boone fetched Milo. It was shallow, what with the man's death, but she couldn't help but realize that all hope of getting her savings had just died, too.

Boone put his arm around her shoulders as they walked to his truck, which was a comfort, but the news was simply too unsettling, for both of them.

"He was a good friend," she said.

"Yeah, he was."

"I'm so sorry, Boone."

He nodded as he opened the rear door for Milo. "Me, too."

They drove back in that zigzag way of his, taking side streets and odd turns. Christie watched him as he checked the mirrors. He had to turn more with one eye swollen shut, and she was sorry she'd ever gotten him involved in this mess. "Did they find anything at Dan's house?"

Boone looked at her, then back at the road. "Not much. No equipment. The only thing that could be something is that he owned a number of properties. One of them isn't far from where you live."

"So you think he set up there?"

"Maybe. It makes sense. He had to have listened from somewhere, and he couldn't have been living in the crawl space."

She thought about that, about how Dan had been in her house. It was worse than the cameras. And now, to find out he'd killed Boone's friend... It was insane. How could he have found out what Larry was doing? Where he lived? Probably the same way he'd gotten to the IRS.

"I've, uh, got some money put aside," Boone said.

"It's not a lot, but it should get you through until you can get back on your feet."

Unexpected tears welled and for a moment she couldn't speak. She wished she'd brought some tissues, but used her thumbs instead, wiping her cheeks as she tried to get it together. After a couple of false starts, she touched his arm. "Thank you, but I'll figure it out. I can always be a waitress. I got through college that way, right?"

"Well, it's there if you want it."

"I appreciate that more than you can know." She leaned over and kissed his cheek.

He grabbed her hand and held on to it until they pulled up in front of her house.

Milo raced to the door and waited impatiently for Christie and Boone. She didn't care. She lingered by the truck until Boone came around. He kissed her, and she wished his mouth wasn't so sore. When his arm came around her shoulders, she leaned into his body, taking comfort while she still could. They walked slowly, in no hurry to get to the trouble ahead. At least they'd had this amazing day. Something she could look back on when Boone was gone.

They walked in together, Milo squeezing between them, making Christie smile. But as the door closed, Milo stopped, ears up, a low growl setting off her internal alarm. She turned to Boone but she stopped dead still. A man, tall, in an expensive looking suit, walked out of her kitchen. He had a gun and it was pointed at her head.

"Stop right there, Garret," the man said, "or she dies."

Christie turned to find another man taking Boone's gun out of his hand, and a third standing in the living room. "Who are you?" she asked, every bit of the terror she'd known coming back, with interest.

"I think your friend Garret knows the answer to that. Why don't you two come in and sit down. And Christie, if you don't control your dog, we will." He gestured meaningfully with his gun.

Christie, shaking and bewildered, got hold of Milo's collar and followed Boone to the couch. They'd left the living room light on before dinner, and the men hadn't turned on any others. She sat as close to Boone as she could and tried to see a way out, but one man, a big guy who looked like a defensive lineman, had them covered from the kitchen door. Another, this one slimmer, but ugly, stood on the other side of the well-dressed man. Both of them had silencers on their weapons, and she could see Boone's gun sticking out of the waistband of the ugly guy's pants.

She turned her attention to the talker. "Who's Garret?"

The man smiled at her, chilling her to her toes. "You mean he hasn't told you? Your boyfriend here isn't Boone Ferguson. He's Garret Edwards, currently wanted by the U.S. government for high treason. Isn't that right, Garret?"

"I know that's a lie," Christie said.

"Of course you do. And I imagine you're going to tell me that you don't know where your brother is." He walked across to the drapes and peeked out between them. When he turned again, his expression had hardened. "So we'll make this easy." He nodded at the man by the kitchen. "Gordon."

Gordon lifted his weapon and before Christie could even gasp, he shot Boone in the thigh. She screamed as

Boone slumped forward, his strangled cry tearing into her like a knife.

"What are you doing?" She let go of Milo's collar to reach for Boone, but the ugly man raised his gun to shoot, and she grabbed Milo before he could get loose. Her dog was insane, barking, lunging at the man who'd shot Boone, but Christie held on.

Boone sat up, his hands pressing tightly on his thigh, which was covered in thick, red blood. He stared at the talking man. "Nate Pratchett is dead."

The man sighed. "My associate has no qualms about shooting your other thigh. Then your kneecaps. Followed by your shoulders. Are we clear?"

"He is dead," Christie said, desperate to make him believe her and leave them alone. "I was there. I saw him die in the explosion with my own eyes."

"Christie, please. Don't be obtuse. We exhumed the bones. We know your brother wasn't killed in that explosion. We also know that he has something that doesn't belong to him, and we want it back."

"That's not true," she said, again.

"Dan," Boone said, his voice tight with pain. "Dan Prescott was your man."

"Very good, Garret. Although some of my colleagues thought his approach was too esoteric, I thought it had merit. And in the end, look what it's brought us. Half your team. I'd say it was quite a success, despite his personal obsession."

"She doesn't know anything," Boone said, his face contorted by old wounds and fresh pain. "She has no idea who any of us are, and she doesn't know a thing about Nate being alive. Let her go. You have me. You got to Larry. And I'm sure you'll find Bill and Jamie, if you haven't already. So let her go."

"Once more, Christie," the talker said, moving toward the other end of the living room. He touched a photograph of her family on the mantel. "Where's your brother?"

"He's buried at the veteran's cemetery in Westwood."

"All right," the man said. "Have it your way." He turned to the man closest to Boone. "Alex, if you would."

Alex took a bead on Boone's other leg, but before he could shoot, Milo ripped his way free and jumped over the coffee table, slamming into the gunman. The weapon dropped as Milo sunk his teeth into the man's wrist.

Christie didn't stop to think—she leapt after Milo, landing painfully on her side. She saw the gun and grabbed it, pointing at Alex, who was hitting Milo with both hands.

"Christie!" Boone shouted and she turned in time to see Gordon aim his gun at her dog. She lifted the weapon and squeezed the trigger twice. With surprisingly little noise, Gordon slid down the wall, leaving a wide smear of blood.

Behind her she heard a shout, and when she turned, Boone was on top of the talking man, his blood staining the expensive suit, and they were struggling, turning, so that even when she pointed the gun again, she didn't dare shoot because she would hit Boone.

Milo's ferocious growls made her turn. The ugly man's face was wet with blood, and he was screaming. Behind her, the man by the kitchen was on the ground, and there was blood there, too.

She had to focus, even though she was dizzy and shaking, and she pointed the gun at the man fighting Boone. In the few seconds she'd looked away, Boone had gotten behind him. He had the man in a hammerlock, and Boone bellowed as he twisted the man's head sharply to the right, the snap so loud she heard it over Milo.

Boone collapsed, writhing as he tried to get the dead weight off him, and then she heard another gunshot, too loud. It was the ugly man. He'd gotten Boone's gun out and was trying to kill Milo. She aimed, but her tears filled her vision and she couldn't see, and when she went to wipe them she heard another shot, and oh, God.

But it wasn't Milo laying still on the floor. It was the ugly man, and the top of his head was blown away. She turned to the front door, to a stranger standing in the shadow, his gun raised. She pointed her weapon, but it was waving so much and she still couldn't see, but she squeezed the trigger—

"Christie. Stop."

She held her finger still at Boone's command.

"Christie," he said again. "Don't shoot. It's Nate."

SHE DROPPED THE GUN AS HER brother walked slowly closer. He'd changed. His hair, which had always been dark like hers was now almost blond, and there were lines by his eyes and mouth that made him look years older. But it was Nate. He was alive.

"Hey, Chris," he said, and then he was hugging her, and she was crying on his shoulder, still not believing that it was really him. "Man, I missed you."

She couldn't talk so she hit his back with both her

fists, the mixture of relief and confusion so strong she felt as if the whole world had gone crazy. "Why? Why did you let me think you were dead?"

"I had to, Chris. I was trying to protect you." He pulled back, and she saw tears on his cheeks. "I didn't do a very good job of it, did I?"

"You bastard. Don't ever do that to me again."

"I'll try real hard not to."

She hugged him again, squeezing hard, but then she thought of Boone, and she broke away.

Boone was still on the floor, pressing his hands into his wound. He was terribly pale. This wasn't good. "Towels," she said over her shoulder. "And an ambulance."

She crouched by Boone. "Baby? Let me help, okay? Can you lay back?"

He shook his head. "Call Harper," he said, his voice just above a croak.

"Okay, we'll call whoever you want, but you need to lay back so I can help. We've got to stop the bleeding, and the bullet might have gone all the way through."

He looked at her with reddened eyes, then with a visible effort, he sat up straighter, wincing in pain she couldn't even imagine.

Nate came back with towels. She gave him a glance when she heard him say, "Hurry," into a cell phone. He dropped the phone next to him and got to his knees. "Let me."

Christie crawled around to Boone's other side, and put her arm around his shoulders. He was heavy as she helped him to his back. She found his hand and squeezed it in hers, praying harder than she ever had before.

Nate cut Boone's jeans off his bad leg. The bleeding didn't look too bad, but the wound was terrible. They rolled him over to look at the underside, and when Christie saw the back of his leg, she knew the bullet had passed through.

Nate, moving so quickly it was almost brutal, wrapped Boone's thigh tightly in two towels, and twisted them together, forming a tourniquet.

"You have any liquor?" Nate asked, not even looking at her.

"Yeah."

"Get it."

She hated to let go of Boone's hand, but she did. She ran to the kitchen, almost tripping over Milo. She got the bottle of bourbon and a glass, and ran back.

Nate threw the glass to the carpet, unscrewed the bottle, and after she got Boone in her arms again, he poured the liquor on the wound. Boone screamed and writhed in her arms.

"Hold him," Nate said. Then he picked up his cell with his bloody hand and punched in some numbers.

"Seth? Get to Christie's. Now." He hung up just as abruptly.

Christie cradled Boone until he stopped moaning, wishing she could do something more. "Should I get some aspirin?" she asked.

"No," Nate said. "It's a blood thinner."

"Where's the ambulance?"

"No ambulance." Nate looked at her. "There's someone coming. Someone we can trust."

"Nate, he could die."

"He won't."

She closed her eyes for a moment, biting back her argument. It wouldn't do any good. All she had to do was look around her to see that there was no point. Their lives were in danger every minute, and there was no place that was safe.

"How did you know?" she asked.

For a second, she thought Nate wasn't going to answer. "I have someone at Omicron."

"What's Omicron?"

"These men, they're Omicron. They're the one's who are trying to stop us."

"Some day you'll have to explain it all to me," she said. "But right now, I think Boone's ready to pass out."

"That might not be so bad. The doc should be here any minute. She wasn't that far away."

Christie bent over Boone. She touched his pale cheek. "You hear that, sweetie? Help's on the way. Just hold on, okay?"

"So, you two…?" Nate asked.

She nodded. "He saved my life. Big-time."

"He's a good man."

"That's what he said about you."

"He's also crazy."

She laughed, but stopped it short, afraid she would start crying again. "You let me think you were dead, Nate. All this time."

"I know. I'm sorry. And I'm even sorrier about what's going to happen next."

She looked at him sharply. "What are you talking about?"

"As soon as Seth and Kate get here, you and I are leaving."

"No."

"Yes. There's no choice in this one, Christie. We're leaving and we're not coming back. You take some clothes, and that's all. Leave your purse, leave your ID, leave it all. You won't need it."

She looked at Boone, his eyes closed now, looking so close to death she had to feel for a pulse. It was there. Weak, but there. "I'm not leaving him."

"You have to."

"No."

"To save both your lives."

"Nate, I can't do that. I can't just walk away from everything."

"Yes, you can. And you will. I'll help you. I'll set you up with a new identity, a new job. We'll get you a place to live. You'll be fine. You just won't be Christie Pratchett anymore."

"What about Mom?"

"You can't call her. Ever."

"Jesus, Nate."

"Would you rather she went to your funeral?"

Christie didn't know what to say. He was asking too much of her. It wasn't fair, none of it. Her home, her life. She'd just gotten it back and now it was being ripped into shreds before her eyes. "The police will be after me."

"There won't be anything here for them to find. No police report will be filed."

"And my house?"

"Will go into foreclosure. It's over. Let it go."

She laughed, then. "Let it go? Let my whole world go? Just like that?"

"It sucks. I'm sorry. But it's your only hope."

She squeezed Boone's hand again. "I want to go with him. Please, Nate."

Her brother, looking so old it broke her heart, shook his head. "Say goodbye, Christie. You don't have much time."

THE CAR DROVE AWAY SLOWLY. Milo had curled up in the back of the dark sedan, and Christie turned in the passenger seat to stare back at her house. There was only the one light in the shaded window, and she couldn't even see shadows behind it, but she knew they were there. The doctor, a woman with strange blue eyes. Seth. Kate. And Boone.

He was alive when she'd stepped out the door, but would he be five minutes from now? Ten?

She'd never see him again. Nate said it would all be over someday, but she didn't believe him. She was lost, as lost as a soul could be. Her heart had been left on a bloody carpet, in a house, in a life she used to love.

19

SHE TURNED OFF THE TELEVISION at nine-thirty. If she could fall asleep by ten, she'd get eight hours of sleep before she had to get back to the restaurant. Even after six months, the work still kicked her butt. The last time she'd been a waitress, she'd been eighteen, nineteen. Now she felt a hundred and nine, and it wasn't getting any easier.

She went into the small bedroom to find Milo had made himself comfy on the queen-size bed. He, at least, could still make her smile. Not much else did.

Her world had become so very small. Work. Meals at home. A book. TV. Sleep. And Boone. He was the largest part of her, now. Thoughts of him filled the empty spaces. Filled her dreams.

All she knew was that he was alive. She chose to believe he was all right, but that's because the alternative made her weep uncontrollably. In her head, he was healthy. Of course, in her head, they weren't really apart. He was just in the next room, or away for the weekend. Then she'd wake up.

"Hey, big guy. You ready to go out?"

Milo got up slowly. His joints didn't like Montana very much. Poor old guy. But he was still the best dog

in the world. She hugged him, then walked with him to
the back door. As always, she turned on the outside
lights and stared through the window to make sure there
was no one there. She scared easily out here, even
though she was in a good part of town. Her neighbors
were a minister and his family on one side, a school
teacher and his wife on the other. Nice folks. She hardly
ever spoke to them.

She let Milo out, and he went into sniff mode immediately. Christie watched him, debating a cup of tea
before she went to sleep. Maybe she'd read a little,
although her attention span sucked.

She wondered, as she did every night, what he was
doing right now. Was he still in the house in Pasadena?
In that awful bed? Of course, now it would be a toss-up
as to who had the most dreary house. But still, if he were
there, that would be a good thing. Because she'd be
able to find him. If...

Milo was done and she let him in. He trotted right to
the water bowl and made his usual mess. She didn't
mind. It gave her something useful to do.

After she mopped up, she filled her teapot and put it
on the stove. It wasn't even her teapot, really. Just
another dollar bargain from the Goodwill. Most everything in here was. Not that she cared. When everything
is stripped away, the important things become very clear.
She wanted Boone. She missed him in a way that hurt.

The whistle made her jump, and she turned down the
fire and got out the tea bags. Her big highlight of the
day—picking out her herbal tea. Tonight, she went with
chamomile.

As she poured the hot water, she heard Milo whine. She stopped pouring, stopped breathing. Milo hadn't whined like that in six months, and the sound pushed her panic button. Carefully, slowly, she put the kettle back down. Walking normally, forcing herself to keep breathing, she went into the bedroom and got her gun from under her pillow. Without even thinking about it, she released the safety. That was the other thing she did here in Bozeman. She went to the shooting range.

Milo was in the living room, and he was staring at the front door. Christie walked up next to him, and touched his head. He licked her hand, then watched the door some more.

A moment later, someone knocked.

She debated ignoring it, but her lights were on. She walked to the side of the door and stood up on her toes. Pulling back the curtain, she looked at the front stoop.

It was a man. A big man with dark hair, and her heart started beating harder. At first glance, from the side, he looked like Boone, but that couldn't be. Boone didn't know where she was. Nate had made sure that no one did. But damn, it sure looked like Boone.

He knocked again, and she saw his profile. A cry escaped as she put the gun down on the table by the door, then jerked the locks open. Her hand shook so hard she almost broke the knob. But then it was open, and oh, God, it was him. "Boone."

He lifted her into his arms, and kissed her over and over, spinning her around and inside, where he kicked the door shut. Then he kissed her again.

He tasted like Boone, like everything she remembered. It wasn't possible, he couldn't be here, but she touched his face and it was *his* face.

"Christie," he said, his voice cracking with emotion. "I can't believe it's you."

She laughed. "That's my line. How are you here? Is it over?"

He studied her eyes as she studied his. So green, so beautiful, with that incredible crease right above his nose. She kissed him right there, and then on the lips again.

He put her down, but she still felt as if she were flying. "Tell me, dammit. How are you here?"

"It wasn't easy. But I found you. Dammit, Christie, I've missed you so much." He swallowed hard. "I had to find Nate first. He didn't want to give it up, believe me. But he told me to tell you to keep the good thought. Things are happening. Slowly, but they're happening."

"So it's not over?"

"No, baby, it's not. We still have a long way to go. But I was miserable without you. If we have to live like this, then I say we do it together. You and me. It won't be fun, but it's not fun now, right?"

She cupped his face. "I knew I loved you for a reason."

"You do, huh? Love me?"

She nodded, so incredibly sure.

"Then you're cool with this? With us?"

She kissed him again, and this time she took her sweet time. It was everything she remembered, and so much more. Her hands explored his back, his butt, then went back for seconds.

When she finally pulled back, he was smiling at her. Not that loopy grin from when his mouth was all banged up, but the beautiful smile she knew from her dreams. "How's your leg?"

"Ugly, but useable."

"Good. That's good."

"No," he said. "This is good. This is worth everything. I love you, Christie. I'm not willing to lose you again."

"Well, isn't that something," she whispered. She touched his lips with her fingertips, then leaned in close. "Because I'm not willing to be lost."

* * * * *

In November 2006, look for Jo Leigh's next
Harlequin Blaze novel, RELENTLESS, part
of an exciting new miniseries featuring
more of Kate, Seth and Nate.

**Hidden in the secrets of antiquity,
lies the unimagined truth...**

Introducing

ROGUE
ANGEL™

a brand-new line filled with mystery
and suspense, action and adventure,
and a fascinating look into history.

And it all begins with DESTINY.

In a sealed crypt in
France, where the
terrifying legend of
the beast of Gevaudan
begins to unravel,
Annja Creed discovers
a stunning artifact
that will seal her destiny.

*Available every other
month starting
July 2006, wherever
you buy books.*

GOLD
EAGLE®

GRA1

Blaze

Sue Johanson's Hot Tips

Forbidden Fantasy #3

Total sexual abandon—
letting him see the real you

Bedroom Bravado

Sexual abandon is all about forgetting your hang-ups and giving in to your primal passion. So liberate yourself with these titillating tips:

Tie the Knot—Literally!
Who says all those scarves in your closet are only winter accessories? Let your lover use them any time of year to tie you up, then give you a loving massage.

A Hands-Free Seduction
A new approach can take your love life from simmering to explosive. The next time you undress him, do it with your teeth! By the time you navigate all his buckles, zippers and buttons, he'll be more than ready to ring your bell!

Learn a New Skill
He'll never complain about "safer sex" when you turn it into a provocative part of foreplay. Shock him by putting a condom on him—with your mouth! It may take a bit of practice, but once you master the technique, he'll never want to go without.

Sue Johanson is a registered nurse, sex educator, author and host of
The Oxygen Network's Talk Sex with Sue Johanson.

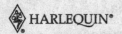